DARK REIGN

AMELIA WILDE

CHAPTER ONE

Emerson

EARLY WINTER. LATE in the day. A good time for the light. In winter the golden hour lasts longer. Makes for better photographs, if you care about that sort of thing. I've never been interested in photos. Not enough tactile interpretation between artist and subject. A click of a shutter, some adjustments in Photoshop—I can hardly find anything evocative in that.

The subjects, however. Anything can be the subject of a photograph, or a painting. Take this city block, for instance. Anyone who is paying attention will notice angles of warm light reaching the sidewalk from the upcoming alley. The soft-stroke cool of deepening shadow. Chill came early this year, but not snow. Brittle leaves cling to patches of concrete. The sun picks and chooses from the dead husks, giving the lucky ones a sheen. Wispy clouds draw the sky closer to the building, the bottoms burnished gold by the sun. Straight-backed skyscrapers interrupt the curves in the distance.

I'm not concerned with that distance. How far the street stretches until it reaches the middle of Manhattan, where those buildings hold back more of the sky. The distance that concerns me now is the number of blocks to my destination.

Six blocks.

Light lingers on a spray of shattered glass in the road. On the other side of the street, a pair of teenagers in puffy coats with the pretentious navy of school uniform slacks underneath point at the breakage. Mild traffic inches around the shards. A dull yellow cab trundles past the opening of the alley. Its color is brought to life for a breath. Then—back into shadow. If this were a painting, this would be the moment to capture. Everything in this little scene is on its way from dark to dark. Ashes to ashes, and all that. But it all spends a singular moment in a slash of sun.

A woman steps out of the alley.

The moment she enters the scene, my perspective shifts. No more teenagers. No more broken bottles. All those unnecessary details distract from the new focus. All discarded in an instant.

She is the subject now, the city street a backdrop for her.

Gold light in black hair. A fine wool coat, nipped at her waist. Her curls lie defined against the dove gray of the wool. Quick steps suggest she knows where she is going. A leather bag bounces against her hip, but she doesn't clutch at it.

She's not afraid.

She could be pretending, I suppose. Pretending that there's no threat to her out here in the street, and in the world. She could be intentionally projecting that she is at ease. Which is it? The way she moves doesn't look like pretending. The purpose of her movement is real, at least. The black-haired woman isn't timid about her steps. She doesn't check her phone for directions. No distractions.

The woman steps out of the light.

I wait for her to recede into the background, now that she's out of all that warmth. All that gold. In shadow, her coat is more heather than dove, but her hair remains the same deep black. In shadow, she is like the sliver of light around a closed door. In a dark room, it's all you can see.

I can't take my eyes off her.

Perhaps it's a conscious decision to follow her. Perhaps not. Either way, I want to know where she's going. I cross the alley. She moves gracefully down the next block. I don't speed up to catch her. A bad idea, when it comes to women on the street. Any change in pace puts them on alert. This woman's petite size works to my advantage. My strides are much longer. No need to hurry.

She checks the traffic at the next intersection despite the white glow of the walk signal. Someone's taught her to be careful. Look both ways. Don't put all your trust in the signals. Maybe that's why she doesn't have her phone in her hand. Though—nothing else in her hands either. No keys in her knuckles. No clenched fists, from what I can see.

The woman steps out, staying in the center of the crosswalk, and reaches the opposite curb.

I have one foot off the sidewalk when a white delivery truck—fading red letters painted on the side in old-fashioned stencil, a rattling muffler—blocks my way.

I can't see her.

The red hand of the walk signal warns me back. *Stop. Stop. Stop.* Well, I've fucking stopped. What more does it want? I brace for an empty sidewalk. No sign of the woman. Gone, as quickly as she appeared.

With a metallic groan the delivery truck lurches forward.

There—she's still there. Moving down the

sidewalk in that way of hers. Almost buoyant, as if the wide street and the towering sky don't bother her.

The signal stops traffic so I can cross. She ducks into an alleyway.

I do not hurry. Measured steps to the alley. The woman is not there. A rusting dumpster huddles against the wall, its edges limned in the golden hour. No petite silhouette. An abandoned chair casts its shadow back at me. Back toward the door. Three-quarters of the way toward the dumpster. Impossible to tell the color in this light. Dark blue, maybe, or slate. There are no other doors on this side of the alley.

Out on the sidewalk, I survey the building. Two stories. Worn brick. Two narrow windows up top, next to a wider bay window. Picture windows below. A sign reads *Motif Gallery*.

I know this place. Rough around the edges. Sells pedestrian art that I don't bother to look at. I attended a showing for a sculptor here ten years ago, before I'd settled on paintings. It's seen better days.

Under no circumstance should I enter this gallery. I've left enough time to walk the requisite fifteen blocks and arrive on time to a private showing in a nearby penthouse. I prefer private showings. Demand private showings. I don't show up at galleries like this one.

My phone vibrates in my pocket. I feel caught out by it, resentful of the fucking thing.

Of course it's my older brother's name on the screen. A prickling cold swerves through my gut and I shove it away. Hit reject. Sinclair can talk to me another time.

I go into the gallery like the phone call was a rude interruption to a fully formed plan. White walls in need of repainting. A creaking blond wood floor. Art that isn't worth the canvas displayed proudly underneath unfilled holes in the drywall. A man behind the counter is absorbed in writing something in a ledger. Probably something extremely fucking artsy, judging by the beret and the black turtleneck. He looks from the screen of his phone to the ledger and back again. Squints. I could ask about her, but I don't want to alarm him. *A woman with black hair in a gray coat. I saw her for fifteen seconds and I want her.*

No, I don't. Curiosity. That's all this is.

I circle around to the other side of the gallery, the other wall.

The painting stops me halfway down, like the shaft of light from the alley. The sidewalk outside, the remaining blocks, and the private showing recede into the background. Details blurred. Irrelevant.

It's a study of an ocean. A subject I've seen thousands of times before—millions—but this one is different. This one makes my heart beat faster. In general, paintings don't do that. A particularly evocative piece will sometimes inspire a distant ache behind my breastbone, a signal that a piece will become or already is quite valuable. This is more. This is closer.

This is all sensation. Spray on my face. Salt on my tongue. Unsteady drifts of sand beneath my feet.

And a dark energy, coiled in the painting. Reaching out for me.

I want to reach back.

I cannot push it away.

I clear my throat until the man in his ridiculous beret approaches. "One of our best pieces."

No shit.

"It doesn't have a price."

"Five hundred." He sticks his hands in his pockets, and I don't like how he's looking at it with me, his shoulder a foot away from mine.

I find the initials of the artist in the lower right-hand corner. *D.M.* The artist should know better. Five hundred dollars is too cheap for this work. Nothing in my galleries costs less than a million, but this is special.

"We'll arrange a private showing."

The man's eyes go up, wrinkling his forehead toward the beret. "Oh, I'm not sure. The artist, she—" Mistake. "We don't normally offer private showings."

No doubt he doesn't. This is a low-end gallery.

"Make an exception." I take my gloves off and fold them into the pocket of my overcoat, following the lines of the brush strokes in the painting. They descend into a roiling darkness that manages to retain its movement even without much suggestion of light. The hairs on the backs of my arms stand up. "Nora likes these kinds of places. She would do a showing here if I mentioned it to her."

He's breathing conspicuously, but I don't look at him. Give the man relative privacy while he realizes who's standing in his gallery. "Which Nora would you be—someone up-and-coming out of Manhattan, or—"

I laugh. "It's not her real name. You must know that by now."

He rubs a hand over his mouth. "Yeah. I do. Everyone knows that."

Everyone knows that Nora is the pseudonym for one of the most popular street artists of the last five years. Famously secretive. Her pieces appear overnight, bursting off walls and billboards and, lately, canvas. It is nearly impossible to schedule a showing with her.

For other people. It's not impossible for me. I've made investments in a few of her pieces because the value will continue to rise.

I meet the man's eyes and find him staring. Frank. Bordering on rude.

"You know her, then." He nods, attempting to keep it casual, but he fails. He's too tense. Overexcited now. He keeps the heat low in this building, which is lucky for him, since he'd be sweating otherwise. A touch to his beret. "And that makes you—you're the Collector. I'm sorry. I should have recognized you. I'm Robert. Owner of the gallery."

"No need for an apology." I'm not often photographed, at showings or otherwise. I've given my release for photographs twice in all my years acquiring art. There's very little for him to go on. I take a business card out of my pocket and press it into his hand. "You'll arrange the showing. And I'll take this painting."

This, at least, is firm ground for him. At the

desk I take a sheet from a notepad and write a message. Fold it twice. "For the artist."

"I'll pass it on." Robert runs my credit card at the machine in his desk, then makes a show of glancing at the business card. "I should contact you at this number?"

"Yes."

"Do you want the painting wrapped?" I give him a look, calibrated to tell this fool in his beret that he needs to keep up without withering him where he stands. "I'll have it delivered."

I shake his hand over the counter. "Nora will hear about your gallery. I'm sure she'll be very excited."

"We'd be honored." He'll be out of his league, is what he'll be. But that doesn't matter. I want this painting, and I want this showing, and I'll get them both.

Leaving the gallery is more difficult than I would have expected. The painting exerts a pull, the way the woman did, and I have the breathless sense that if I waited, I would find her at that painting.

Foolish. Allowing myself to feel for this long—it's foolish. Reckless. I don't want these emotions close enough to name, but there they are.

One of them is hope. It's a bright spot in a dark space, surrounded by heat and violence and memory. Emotions are best kept pinned down. Held at arm's length.

But this painting—

This woman—

On the sidewalk I feel the pinprick awareness that someone has taken notice.

Curiosity turns my head. I half-expect to see her standing there in her gray coat, exposed to the fast-approaching night. But the sidewalk is empty, except for an empty newspaper vending machine and a streetlight. A stray piece of paper blows past in the breeze and slaps the gallery window like it's trying to get inside. Again, that pull—*go back to the painting. Don't leave it behind.*

Another tug.

This time, to the second floor.

We've lost more of the sun since I went in. A weaker glow from those narrow windows pushes into the evening. The competing light from outside makes it possible to see a set of lace curtains. Still. Serene. Undisturbed.

The curtains, and the shadow of a woman behind them.

CHAPTER TWO

Daphne

WE GET A few visitors to the gallery every day, but most of them don't buy anything. People stop by to see Robert, the owner, and in the winter they stop in to warm up from the cold. Sales could be better. That's what Robert always says. He's trying a new technique lately—giving people plenty of space to get attached to the art.

This visitor has to be a good sign. It's close to closing, but he was here long enough to buy something.

When the door closes I go to my window to peek through the lace. He's walking away. Long strides. A dark coat. That's all I get.

And then, as if he senses me watching, he turns his head.

I freeze behind the curtain and avert my eyes. I don't know what I'm thinking, trying to catch a glimpse.

Three ringing *bang*s startle me back into motion. It's Robert, banging on the ceiling of the gallery—my floor—with a stick, like he does when he wants to go on a lunch break. One more look at the sidewalk. Nobody's there now, only a couple with their arms linked. On the way to dinner, maybe. Across the street is a building almost identical to this one. Both of them were built at the same time. The difference is that the bottom floor of that building is a tiny grocery store.

The top floor is an apartment. That's where my security team stays. My brother Leo wants them closer, but there's no room. His "compromise" was to buy the building across the way and keep the space open for the people on the team. Dark windows watch me back. I like it better when the lights are off. I can pretend I'm on my own.

There's one way out of my apartment. My door opens on a strangely wide hallway. The downside is that my apartment could be bigger if it weren't for the hall, but the upside is that I can move bigger canvases in and out when I need to. A dusty landing at the bottom of the stairs leaves me between two doors. One leads out to the alley. The other leads into the back room of the gallery.

"You rang?" I call to Robert, stepping through. "Or—pounded, I guess."

"He bought your painting." Keys jangle at the front door. He's locking up. I push aside the beaded curtain separating the crowded back room from the gallery.

"What?"

"Yeah." Robert turns around, blinking. He rubs a hand over his beret. "He wants it shipped. Paid extra for that."

"Why do you look so weird?"

He shakes his head, fast, like he's shaking off his shock. "Because he's the Collector."

I can hear the capital C in his voice. My heart speeds up. Anyone who has a title like that is good for the gallery. And if he bought my painting—"Who's the Collector?"

Robert comes around behind the counter and sits heavily on the tall stool there. "Super rich. Loves art. Has a collection that could rival MoMAs. Extremely discerning." A sidelong glance at me. "I've never seen him here, but he wanted your piece. He looked at it like—" Robert laughs. "I don't know, Daph. Like he might have fallen in love with it."

My cheeks go hot. That's the dream—having someone fall in love with my paintings. Someone other than me, anyway. I catch myself about to tug the collar of my shirt and lean casually against the counter instead. "Fallen in love?" My heart is in my throat. "That sounds intense."

"He paid full price." Robert raises his eyebrows at me, perching both hands on his beret.

"No way."

"I'm serious."

People don't pay full price at Motif. They don't. Robert's better at haggling than I am. Talking about money seems like an opening for people to get into intrusive questions.

"So what you're telling me is that a man walked into the gallery, saw my painting, fell in love with it...and handed you five hundred dollars?"

"The Collector. Not just anyone. And then the weird thing—" A short, high laugh escapes me. This is all weird. This is all weird. I never imagined that someone would feel the way I do about one of my paintings. I feel intense when I paint them. Dark and intense and nothing at all like I'm supposed to be, which is sweet and innocent and safe. "You okay?" Robert asks.

"Tell me what the weird thing was."

"He left you a note."

"Me?"

"For the artist, he said." Robert pushes a piece of paper across the counter. It's from the notepad he keeps next to the credit card machine. There's no casual way to read it in front of him, so I shoot for serious. I clear my throat, stand up straight, and unfold the note.

Crescent Cove beach at twilight

The handwriting's neat. Strong. Controlled. It reads like a request for a meeting. An order for a meeting, really. But—no. The Collector must be saying he wants me to paint the ocean at this spot. I've never heard of this place before. Even if I had, I might not be able to call its location to mind before.

What he's written is more intimate than a request for a meeting. It's a commission, and people don't commission paintings of places that are meaningless to them.

"What did he write?" Robert lifts his chin to look over the edge of the paper. I pull it to my chest on instinct. Good for me. I've made this message look even more illicit and interesting.

"Nothing." I tuck it into my pocket and return Robert's wide-eyed stare. "Same thing you said. He loved the piece."

"He really wanted to make sure you knew, then." Robert folds his arms over his chest and looks at my painting. "I think he would have paid double the price." Another shake of his head. "When you're here tomorrow, maybe you could spend some time thinking about the prices. It could be good if we bumped them up. If you feel like it."

"No, sounds good. I'll look at the listings, make sure everything's up to date—"

"Make some sales…"

"And hopefully make some sales."

Robert grins at that, and then he pats his knees and stands up in the universal signal for I'm going home. "See you tomorrow afternoon, Daphne. Congrats on the sale."

He holds up his hand for a high five, and I give him one. It seems right. I sold a painting today. At full price.

I'm on a semi-complicated cloud nine on the way back up to my apartment. This warm, floaty feeling—that's success. I made someone feel something, and the only way they could think to respond was by making my art their own. With the money I make from the sale I'll be able to buy more canvas and paint and put something else on the wall at the gallery. A bigger piece, maybe. A higher price. I've sold a few small pieces since I graduated, but not many. All of them were much smaller. All of them were more careful work. I didn't put as much of myself into those.

I flip the lock on the door and try to hold on to the victory. Because it is a victory, even if it's not the fully independent victory I'm aiming for.

Robert takes a twenty-five percent commission on my pieces. He takes fifty from everyone else but flatly refuses to take more from me. So I'll get more money from the sale than another person at the gallery on top of the Collector paying full price.

And then there's the rent.

I sink down into my couch and rest my head. The couch was a castoff when Eva decided to re-do her apartment last, so it's cream leather and completely out of my budget. I try my best to live off what I make at the gallery. The arrangement I have with Robert is to take a tiny hourly rate for my shifts in exchange for the apartment.

And both those things—the reduced commission and the apartment—are because I'm not Daphne, girl with a fine art degree trying to make her way in the world. It's because I'm Daphne Morelli.

I'm the second-youngest daughter in a family that was ruled by my father, Bryant, until my oldest brother Lucian took over. It was a whole thing that led to many bristling silences at family dinners until Lucian laughed and changed the subject. When Robert looks at me, he doesn't see me, the artist. He sees my father lurking in the background. Lucian, with all the power of Morelli Holdings behind him, and a reputation for cold calculation and colder vengeance. He's never hurt me, but sometimes, when he thinks no one's paying attention, I can see how much he'd rather be taking people apart to see what makes them tick.

But people like my father or Lucian or even my oldest sister pale in comparison to Leo.

I know what people say about him. I heard whispers at school. By my senior year of college, Leo had become a subject of debate. On the one hand, he's been known for a long time as the Beast of Bishop's Landing—a snapping, snarling person who won't control his temper and uses his rage against people. *He's violent,* a girl whispered once in an oil painting seminar. *I heard he kills people on the way into the office every morning.* The person she was talking to laughed. *That's not what I've heard. I've heard he's a rich asshole who's good at real estate, like all the rest of them. My dad signed a deal with him last week. Said it was fine.*

Never mind the city's conflicted views on what he's actually like. Leo wasn't about to let his reputation stand between me and the rest of the city. He came here himself.

On my move-in day he visited the gallery and interrogated Robert. Then he came upstairs and stalked between the rooms until I thought I'd lose my mind. He finally stopped at my window and looked down at the street.

He wasn't happy. He was worried. I could see it in the way he stood, tall and tense, scanning the traffic below. Guilt gnawed at my insides. I wanted to tell him I'd changed my mind. That he could find me another place. He's my favorite brother. I wanted to make him happy. It would have been easy.

"It's not that bad of a neighborhood," I'd said.

He looked me in the eye with the same focus he'd used to watch the street, his dark eyes a match for mine. "Are you sure you want to live here?"

Yes. I was sure then, and I'm sure now. The very next day a crew arrived at the building across the street. They gutted the apartment on the second floor. They hadn't been finished for five minutes when the security team started setting up. This is the one thing Leo won't compromise on, no matter how many times I tell him I'm perfectly safe here. The team stays.

Eva doesn't understand why I want this place so much. Guilt expands in my throat. I've said no to them so many times since I graduated in May, but they can't—or won't—stop asking. Eva offers me a spare bedroom. Two spare bedrooms, if I want a studio. And Leo offers more money. Apartments overlooking Central Park. My own gallery. He doesn't want me to worry about money.

It would be nothing to him. I know. He could support me for the rest of my life and never feel a pinch, because my brothers are awash in money. They wield it like they wield power. They're confident in it. It's theirs.

I want my own. My own money. My own apartment. My own way in the world. Anything else feels like drowning.

The heat kicks on, rustling my lace curtains. My two rooms plus bathroom are small and dusty, big enough to paint in but not much else, and I love it here. I love the knitted blanket I keep on the back of the couch and the tea kettle I got at an antique store and the bay window in the bedroom. I wedged a full-size mattress at the very back so I'd have more room for my easel and all my paints.

I breathe through the nagging guilt. It's worse

whenever I feel irritated by my siblings, especially Leo, especially the things he does to keep me safe. They're not new. He's been protecting me for as long as I can remember. And not from imagined threats. From very real people who lived in our house.

Enough of that. I've had a request for a commission.

I take out my phone, pull the blanket over my lap, and google the beach. Send my brother a text.

Daphne: I sold a painting today!!

I do not send a second text about the note. It feels wrong not to tell him, but telling him will turn this into a big deal.

Crescent Cove turns out to be a cove—pretty on the nose—with a tiny stretch of public beach in the middle surrounded on either side by private beaches. It's a fancy little town about an hour away. Nothing dangerous about it. The beach will be empty this time of year. Perfectly safe.

Leo: You'll be world-famous by spring.

A commission. I got a commission today. I'm ordering dinner for that. It's worth celebrating. Dinner and Netflix, and tomorrow, a trip to the beach.

CHAPTER THREE

Emerson

THE REPORT ON my painter arrives in my inbox at the same time the painting arrives on my doorstep. A man in a thick, Army-green coat wraps his hands around the sides of the canvas, squeezing tight to keep it from falling. I don't want him touching it. Not even through the protective wrapping. I step back to let him into the foyer.

"Where do you want it?" His eyes dart around the room, but there's nothing to see. The entry table and matching chair in a dark cherry wood that warms in afternoon light. My dining table in the space to his left. The closed doors to a study. Behind us is the living room, but he won't be going there. I don't allow the impatience to grow. It's expected, of delivery people, that they can't control their need to stare.

"Here is fine." He steadies it against the entry table and turns back. I already have his tip in hand. Another person has been in my space too long, and the email taunts me from the top of my inbox. Curiosity is a dry scorch at the back of my throat.

I don't give in.

Yet.

The delivery man steps out onto the porch. When the door's locked behind him, I move to the dining room window. The truck starts with a rumble, and he guides it around the circle drive and toward the gate. It opens for him, and only when it's closed again do I allow myself to return to the painting.

I take it into the dining room and remove the coverings. It's a mid-size piece, perhaps four feet across. I brace myself against any emotion at all. It's possible, though not likely, that I will feel differently about the piece now that it's here. Now that it's mine.

The last of the wrapping falls away.

It's like being slapped in the face with a cold wave. That ache I felt in the gallery is back. More intense now. I push all of it to the side and try to look at the painting without expectation. I can't do it. What I felt—it was real. It takes a minute to get myself under full control. To stop thinking of those slashes of light at the edges of a doorframe, searching for a way in.

I lay the dark-magic canvas down on the dining room table and leave the room.

Lucky for me, the information I need has already arrived. It's waiting for me. The person who made this painting, who reached into my soul and shook it, is waiting for me. I keep my mind carefully blank on the way into my study. No expectations.

The image of the woman's shadow behind her lace curtain floats weightlessly across my memory.

The artist, she—

A slip-up on Robert's part. A woman. That's all I know. Whoever painted this could be any woman in the city. In the world. I sit down at my desk and jiggle the mouse to wake up my computer. This is one report I want to read in full definition. Not on a cramped phone screen.

The email springs open at the first click. Scroll. I ignore whatever comments my man in the city has left and open the report itself.

Daphne Morelli, artist's signature: D.M.

Seven photos of her initials on various pieces accompany this bit of information, and a photo of her. There are more photos. The urge to scroll down and devour them is strong, but I won't. This is important. This requires patience, and attention.

Daphne Morelli is the daughter of Bryant and Sarah Morelli out of Bishop's Landing.

My perspective shifts again. I arrive at the first photo that's not of her artist's signature.

It's her. The woman from the street. Same black hair. Same lines of her body. A strange relief. I wanted her, and now she's been delivered to me in this email. Yesterday, she was a woman on the sidewalk in a gray coat, but now she has depth. The photo is her last school ID. It turns out that her hair isn't black—it's a very dark brown, with dark eyes to match. Tiny chips of gold in those eyes. She grins in the photo, completely at odds with what everyone knows about her family.

The Morellis are infamous. In Bishop's Landing. In the city. Everywhere. They are a nebulous danger that people talk about with their eyebrows slightly raised, as if to telegraph the risk of dealing with the Morelli family. Not financial risk, though there's always an element of that in anything worth doing. They mean—don't piss them off. Attack one Morelli, attack them all. A bit of a dynasty, unlike my brothers and me. They're more like the Constantines, another wealthy family with whom they are in a constant petty rivalry. I suspect most of the rumors about the Morellis come from the Constantines, but I don't particularly care.

Daphne doesn't look dangerous. She looks innocent. Hopeful, I would say. Hopeful, rather than cynical and hard. Odd for a person with her last name. It must have been cultivated in her, that sweetness. Guarded somehow. Twenty-three, and she still has that light in her eyes. That light—it's hiding something, if her painting is any indication.

Daphne graduated from NYU in May. Bachelor of Fine Art. Her student exhibitions have been included, but I move past them. The painting I saw wasn't a student piece. She was still finding herself when she was in college. Her first paintings of the ocean happened toward the end, and they were quick studies.

Current residence is above the Motif Gallery. One-bedroom apartment.

By the alley? Why would a Morelli want to live in such a shitty place? It's barely clean. Definitely not secure. The Morellis run billion-dollar businesses. Their daughter doesn't need to set foot in a place like the Motif Gallery.

More photos of her. College photos, mainly. Daphne in the studio, with her hair pulled up on top of her head, laughing as she paints. Daphne accepting an award at an end-of-school banquet, grinning. But it's the last photo that freezes my hand in place and sends blood rushing to my cock.

Daphne, standing alone outside a shop somewhere in the city. A paparazzi photo. Someone was going to try and make money off the Morellis and lost his nerve. The photo isn't particularly titillating. Not worth the cost of provoking the Morelli institution. The photographer's name is printed below the photo, along with a notation—*sold to Morelli Holdings. Unpublished.*

It's the expression on her face that arrests my attention.

My painter comes from a rich family, but her expression is filled with longing. She is looking past whatever is in that shop window. I doubt she sees it at all. In the cool shadow of the building, she is in waiting. Waiting for the sun to touch her face. Waiting to be lit up with possibility. Longing for it.

I want to create that expression on her face the way she puts the living ocean on canvas. I want to feel it in her body. Watch it pour out of her and become something else.

Art.

Fierce desire bolts through me, spine to toes,

concentrating in my cock. Fuck. *Make it specific. Put it in terms that can be controlled.*

I want to watch emotions scrawl themselves across her face, her eyes, her mouth. I want to witness the transfer of that emotion from body to canvas. I want to watch it become. Right now, Daphne Morelli's tears and thoughts and feelings are a black box. I've seen her. I've felt the results. Ocean spray on my face. Salt on my tongue. Between the longing in her eyes and the first stroke of the brush is a void. A veiled mystery. I want it uncovered.

Of course, there is an antecedent to all this— her family. My man has included information about them, too. A series of press photos taken at a gala last year.

There are her parents. Bryant and Sarah. Bryant has the dark-haired look about him, those same dark eyes, and his smile is more of a glare. Handsome and fit, despite being in his sixties. His wife is a redhead. Petite. Distant. Her mind is elsewhere while the cameras flash. She stands close to his side. I wonder if she does that when no one's watching.

The next photo is a group shot. *Lucian Morelli. Eva Morelli. Sophia Morelli. Lisbetta Morelli.* A short paragraph underneath sketches out the details. *Lucian Morelli, eldest son. CEO at Morelli Holdings. Recently replaced Bryant Morelli at the helm. Eva Morelli, second eldest. Lives in Manhattan. Sophia Morelli. Second daughter, sixth child. Lisbetta Morelli. Youngest child. Boarding school.*

There she is—in the next set of photos. Two of them. Daphne laughs at a man dressed all in black—black tux, black shirt. Custom, from the look of the tailoring. He's tall, lean, black-brown hair that matches hers.

He's touching her. Jealousy surges. His hand on her back. From the angle of his arm, his palm is low on her shoulders, and her elbow brushes his side as she laughs. He wears an amused smile, captured as he speaks to her. In the next frame, they both look out at the cameras. Her eyes are bright, as if they'd shared a private joke.

They seem close. My jealousy is causing a physical reaction now, one I don't like, and I take several breaths and scroll to find out who this motherfucker is.

Leo Morelli. Second son, third child. Owns a subsidiary of Morelli Holdings in Manhattan. Real estate. "Beast of Bishop's Landing." More detail upon request.

Her brother.

The jealousy subsides, but it's replaced with something else. Awareness. Of this brother, yes, but all of them. They're distinct faces now. Except—

I scroll back up. Daphne has seven siblings in total. Four brothers, three sisters. Two of her brothers weren't at the gala, but other photos have been included.

Tiernan Morelli. Third son. Works for Bryant Morelli.

The photo of him is grainy. It shows a distinctive scar on his face.

Carter Morelli. Fourth son. Graduated from Oxford. Lives overseas.

So the youngest child at boarding school was flown home for this event, but not Carter. There is a dynamic in play. I would guess, from the photos, that one of the older brothers is at the center of it. Lucian, perhaps. Or—Leo, from the way Daphne laughed at him. It's a single frame but it's genuine.

My phone buzzes on the desk where I've abandoned it. My thumb is already above the reject button when the name registers. Will. My younger brother. The photo of Daphne with her brother, laughing at him, happy with him, lands at the center of my screen.

"Yeah?"

"Hi to you too, Emerson." Will's going somewhere. He's always going somewhere. There's birdsong in the background. Central Park, maybe, on his way to somewhere else. Winter birds. Probably the building where he headquarters his tech startup. "Did Sin call you?"

"I didn't answer."

"Asshole."

"Did you want something?"

"No, but Sin does." A laugh, punctuated with more birdsong. "He wants us to get together. He wants us to be one big, happy family. I told him the odds weren't great, given everything."

Everything encompasses our shitshow of a childhood, which is kept in its own box, out of sight, out of mind. The memories fight against their frames. I pull up the app on my desktop that shows me the security system for the house. All the doors are locked. Two deep breaths to push away the sensation of a threat.

"That ship has sailed," I tell Will.

"Sin said something about new beginnings." He sounds thoughtful. "I think he might be fucking someone new."

"He's always fucking someone new." I scroll down past the gala photos to a larger collection of

Daphne herself. Anything he could find, plus more details from her life. She won a fellowship at NYU. Graduated with honors. Did well at the private Catholic prep school she attended. It's not enough. It's all the information I requested and then some, and it's still not enough.

No one captivates me in this way. People are always trying to talk to me about new, emerging artists, and for the most part I'm not interested. Nora is an exception. I made my money on the masters throughout history, and built my collection from them, too. New is exciting for small minds. I'm in the business of depth. I'm in the business of excellence.

Something in Daphne's painting spoke of both.

And the woman herself—

"Are you listening to me?" Will asks.

"No."

"Sin said he's coming to New York."

I don't like that. No wonder Will didn't stop to harass me about not listening to his bullshit. This is a call with a purpose.

"Why?"

Will huffs. "Why do you think?"

"Christ." The last thing I need is my older brother trying to make amends. Some things can't be repaired. Once you take a knife to canvas, it doesn't matter how well you paint over the gash—it will never be the same. "You don't think he'll try to stay with me?"

"Why?" Will mocks. "Is your eight-thousand-square-foot beach house not big enough for the two of you?"

No. It's not, but I can't tell my brother that. We grew up in the same situation, but the three of us—we're not the same.

They like open spaces.

CHAPTER FOUR

Daphne

THE LIGHTS ARE on early in the security apartment when I order the Uber. They're changing shifts, probably. Or watching. I ignore them when the car pulls up to the sidewalk. I check the license plate, check the driver's face, and get in.

"It's cold out for the beach." He glances at my sketchpad in the rearview mirror.

"I have a commissioned piece," I tell him, and I can't keep the smile off my face. "They picked the place. I have to paint it. It's a pretty big deal."

"Good for you."

I open my mouth to tell him more. Then—"Thank you. I love this song. Can you turn it up?"

It's best to err on the side of keeping information to myself. Staying quiet, in my experience, is safer than spilling your guts to anyone who seems ready to listen. And it's not that I don't want a voice—I do. But part of being an independent woman is knowing when not to speak.

This Uber driver doesn't need to hear about my feelings, anyway. I'm excited about the commission, and torn. I should definitely ignore the note. But I'm too curious about this rich old guy who bought my painting. He probably has white hair. Or is balding. In his fifties, or even older. Those are the kinds of men who have money to buy paintings like mine in a casual way. An old man would probably like this stretch of beach and find it interesting. We listen to music all through the ride, which is where I make a compromise in my head.

Leo wouldn't want me to be here. The security team didn't follow me in their black SUV, but I bet they took down the license plate of the Uber. I climb out and go around to the driver's side window. "Can I pay you to stay here and wait for me? I shouldn't be more than an hour."

I have money for this. A hundred dollars left over from the sale of my painting. I also have an emergency credit card from Leo, but I won't touch that.

"Hell yeah," he says. He's younger than I thought and peers dubiously at the beach behind me. "Just order another ride when you're done. I'll stay right here."

"Fifty now, fifty when I get back." I hand him the first bill and he gives me a thumbs-up.

The road where he's parked is raised above the beach. A stone staircase bisects a retaining wall. A cold salt taste saturates the air, with more frost packed into the sand. The snow's not sticking yet but chill radiates through my boots. Pale sunlight sinks below a cool purple sky.

Crescent Cove beach at twilight

Waves roll against the sand in time with my footsteps. The sand crunches like snow under my feet. A lone beach chair has been left out, and that's where I go.

My phone buzzes.

Eva: Free for dinner?

Daphne: Painting tonite. What about Saturday?

I should have brought a blanket. If that Uber driver keeps his word, he'll make a hundred dollars for way less than an hour. My heart hammers under my layers. The breeze toys at the winter hat Eva gave me for Christmas last year—a cashmere beanie that's good for walking from class to my apartment. Not quite enough for drawing on the beach when it's this cold.

Eva: It's a date! My place at 7?

Daphne: Bad movies ONLY

Eva: ;)

Okay. Bag. Pencil. Sketchpad. I open my book to a fresh page. At least my coat is warm enough to do a quick sketch. I need a sense of the place before I can paint.

So this is going to be the hard part of a commissioned piece. Keeping the Collector out of my head when I paint. Whoever he is, he wants my interpretation of it. My graphite tip hovers over the page. Mine. No one else's. No asking for instructions. No assignment rubric, the way they had in school. Just me, my sketchbook—

And someone else.

A surfer out in the water.

I don't surf, so I can't compare the size of the waves. Medium-sized. He's a tall silhouette against the purple-gold twilight sky. My pencil moves, capturing the shape of the wave, the movement. It's carrying him toward the shore. Toward me. And then his body shifts backward, no hesitation, all grace, and he's under the water.

Oh, god, it has to be so cold. Cold enough to freeze a person, wetsuit or not. Right? But he's back up before I can wonder anymore. Paddling out and out and out so he can catch another wave.

This one, he takes all the way back to the sand.

I make a few more sketches, but it's not the shape of the waves I'm drawing anymore. It's the loneliness of a man out there by himself in all that water. The aching sweep of the sky. Dark water. Dark wetsuit. He could have disappeared, if he wanted.

The man unhooks himself from the board and tucks it under his arm. It's hard to breathe, with his body in a wetsuit. Shit—he might think I'm drawing him in his wetsuit.

"I wasn't drawing you," I blurt out when he reaches my chair.

He stops. Looks down at me. It's hard to tell what color his hair is in this light, and when it's wet—light, but not very. Maybe a sandy blond. Can't tell the color of his eyes, either. He's all shape and form. Strong shapes. Sharp forms. "What are you drawing, then?"

"The ocean." I turn the sketchbook around to show him. To prove it. My face heats. It's meaningless swirls at this point. The feeling of it. The sensation. Notes on the sensation, really— reminders, for when I start painting. Color is what adds depth. The pencil swirls probably look ridiculous, but he considers them seriously. "It's for a commission."

"You're an artist."

I shrug. I never know what to say to this question. The answer is yes, but if I say that, he'll ask if he's seen my work. He'll want to know if I've been featured anywhere, which—no. I'm a starving artist with a full stomach thanks to my brother and my sister. "I like it."

"It's good."

My laugh comes out as more of a snort. "It's preliminary sketches. It has to be good when it's done, though." For the first time, I feel the pressure of this moment. Of the Collector loving my piece. This is my first commission. No one's ever ordered one before. In a way it's the most important painting of my life, so I'm here trying to get the idea."

Another glance at my sketchbook, and then he looks back to the ocean. "You captured the mystery of it."

This tiny praise makes my chest light up. This man has no idea who I am. He's not saying it because I'm Leo's sister or Bryant's daughter or part of a family dynasty with a surplus of power. "I think it's more mysterious that you're out here surfing. I thought people did that in, you know, warm weather."

"I surf as long as there are waves. It's a good wetsuit." He slides the board next to my chair. I didn't notice the black backpack in the sand before. He's efficient with the zippers, pulling out a jacket that unfolds from nothing and a plastic rectangle. He puts the coat on over his wetsuit and opens the plastic. Unfurls it out into the dying light. Silver flashes. "For you."

I catch a corner of it out of the air. A loud, crinkling catch. "A blanket?"

"For emergencies." He takes a towel out of the backpack and dries his hair.

"I'm totally fine."

He shoots me a look, and there's a warmth in it. A familiar exasperation. "Your knees are shaking."

It's not because of the cold, but I tuck the blanket around my lap anyway. "There. No more emergency."

He sits down on the surfboard. My chair is so low, and he's so much taller, that we're on the same level. More waves roll in. My muscles are tight with awareness of him. With how close he's sitting.

"Aren't you cold?" I ask.

"Aren't you supposed to be sketching?"

I laugh at his joke, but I adjust my grip on the

pencil and flip to a new page. The ocean is different when someone is sitting at my side. The whole scene is different—the feeling. Ocean droplets feel less like tiny chips of glass and more like snowflakes. Meant to wake me up, not to hurt. I'm not going to get hurt out here. If he was going to do it, he'd have done it already. He wouldn't have given me a blanket.

It's not the safest situation ever. I recognize that. But the Uber driver is waiting for me. A couple minutes sketching in earnest and my mind settles. It falls into the shapes on the page and building up the memory of the way the ocean is now. Darker by the minute. Soon the sky and the sea will be the same deep shade. Moonlight on the water will set them apart.

"They'll like it."

I'd gotten used to the crash of the waves, and the man's silence in it. "Who?"

"Whoever commissioned the piece. What you're doing here is completely different from the sketch you made before."

"A few minutes makes a difference," I say, hoping I sound sage and smart and not self-conscious. "That's why the ocean is such a good subject." This is a bit of a hedge. It's the only subject I'm interested in lately. For months and months. "It changes all the time. Becomes something else."

I meet his eyes over the arm of the chair. He's nodding. Agreeing with me. Not in a patronizing way, either. His perfect lips part, gaze slipping down. He might ask me out. He might ask for my number. Men have asked before, but I always say no. If he asked, I would say yes.

"You have sand on your nose," he murmurs, and he reaches for me.

I flinch.

I can't help it. Can't stop it. He freezes, his hand inches away. His face is transformed, like the ocean. Flirtation to concern. A flicker of something else, maybe. He lowers his hand. "Someone hurt you."

He's not a fan of questions, this man. *You're an artist. Someone hurt you.*

More waves splinter on the sand. They're a better place to look. "Everyone gets hurt at one point or another. That's how you learn about power. Someone uses it against you. And then, eventually, it comes out onto canvas."

"Like Lehmann's paintings, right? That famous one. *Where the Ocean Meets Sky.*" The smile I put on my face is tense. Fake. It matches cold disappointment in my gut at hearing the mention of a dead, terrible man. A celebrated artist, and a monster. He liked painting the ocean, too. We studied his pieces in school, and I can't tell you how many times I've been compared to him. "What's wrong?"

"Nothing." I relax my fingers around the pencil. Holding it in a tight grip makes it harder to draw. No good for anything. But my fingers are getting stiff.

"You don't like his work."

"His work is technically sound. He has an eye for color and light."

"Then what?"

A soft laugh bubbles up. "Sometimes it's hard to separate the artist from the art."

This beautiful man, in his coat and his wet-suit, arches an eyebrow. "And Lehmann can't be separated."

"You know, all the information is out there. He didn't try to hide how he beat his wife." My voice has gone flat, but I can't help that either. I can't show emotion when I talk about this, otherwise it'll come out—the broken part of me, from my own father. He didn't get to me often. It was enough. Everything happened behind closed doors at our house while my father got accolades at church for being such a good Catholic. "His wife, his children. Anyone who got in his way. Everyone knew, and no one cared. The German government awarded him with a national art prize and made him the head of that art department. They didn't care."

I've said way too much. I'm almost sick with it, but I look anyway. Nervousness rises that he'll judge me for caring, or worse, agree with society that it's not a big deal.

But he looks thoughtful. "People care. People who know better." He stands up from the surfboard. "Do you have a way home?"

The Uber is still waiting for me at the top of the rise. "Who said I was done sketching?"

"Your hands are too cold to draw." He looks around. Spots the car. "For you?"

"Yeah." I don't want this conversation to be over. I want to listen to him talk all night. You could never capture this voice in a painting—it's too fine for that, too gorgeous. But he's right about my hands.

He offers me his. He's got big, steady hands. "I'll walk you. Let's go."

CHAPTER FIVE

Emerson

ROBERT WELCOMES ME into the gallery like he's been waiting for me. He has. He and his beret have had two weeks to make Motif more acceptable. I've come after closing through fresh, dark night. Robert closes the door behind us and locks it. Flips the sign. He's busy with it while I put my gloves in my pocket. "Mr. Leblanc. It's an honor to have you back. If you'll come this way…"

This way, as if the place is big enough to need directions. Daphne's pieces are obvious. Two of them, side by side, in the center of the left-hand wall.

Not the display wall in the middle of the gallery.

I have to walk past an irrelevant piece to get to her paintings. The cutting comment I was about to make drowns in Daphne's work.

Sensation pours out of them, so much so that I have to step closer. To see each one in turn. One is of the ocean at daybreak. The light from above doesn't penetrate to the bottom of the canvas, but she hasn't used flat black. I have the impression of movement. A creature lurks out of sight of the sun. Something's down there. Something's coming. Light outlines a door. Unseen danger on the other side. In Daphne's painting, the sun will rise soon. Nowhere to hide.

And the second.

I don't take my hand out of my pocket and put it to my chest, but I want to.

There is no beach in the painting, but I recognize the particular curves of the waves from that night. Twilight bleeds into dark water, the colors like an oil slick on the surface. Part of the surface. Heavy purple and palest orange refract over infinitesimal peaks. My heart has escaped its bounds. A casual observer might think this was similar to the first piece I bought, or even the one next to it, but it is not. The water rushes out toward the sky, not in toward the viewer. An undertow. And something out of the frame is causing a disturbance. No. That's the wrong word. Something else, unseen to the viewer, is influencing the water. The shadow of his indentation reaches onto the canvas from the bottom.

Like a man on a surfboard.

She hasn't painted her interpretation of the ocean at Crescent Cove beach at twilight. She's painted mine.

This view is the one I force myself to see over and over and over again. Once a day, ideally. More if necessary.

Only on this canvas, the sight takes on new meaning. There's mystery here. Possibility. Hope.

My painter was soft as the light faded. Delicate and vulnerable. Almost luminescent, as if a statue could be made from mother-of-pearl.

Robert comes back into my awareness. He's been hovering in silence, pretending to see what I see in these pieces. He sees nothing. The painting hanging on the display wall is proof of that.

"I'd like to see the artist."

He takes a step back, his hand coming up to his beret. "I'm not sure if that's—we don't do many private showings, but I've always thought it might leave an appropriate distance if—"

"Nora likes the sound of your gallery. She'll be back in the US later this week, and will be making a stop. Her pieces arrive twenty-four hours in advance, and her people will collect them as soon as the showing is over."

He swallows. If he gives me what I want, it

will be a coup for the gallery. Nora, as it happens, always draws a crowd. There won't be pieces to take with her at the end of the showing and the Motif Gallery will see an outrageous commission. A badly needed commission, if the rundown facade of this place is anything to go on.

"If you'll give me a minute. She lives near here. I can't guarantee—" He thinks better of it. "One minute."

His strides are quick on the way to the back. "Hi," he says as the beaded curtain rattles back into place behind him. "Remember the piece you sold?" A nervous laugh. "Okay, I know. Listen. I arranged a private showing with the buyer. He's here now, and he's requesting to see you."

Robert's voice drops. Not enough, in a place like this, with all the cheap wood and open space. "That's—I know. I couldn't schedule a private showing in the middle of the day when we might have someone trying to get in. Yes. No. It's perfectly safe."

A long pause. The ache in my chest from her piece intensifies. If I didn't know better I would call it desperation. It's criminal that I can't hear what she's saying. Ridiculous that I can't see her already. I know where she is. She's right above my head. Sitting on her bed, or waiting by the door.

She's not pacing the floor.

"It'll be really good for the gallery, Daph." The familiar nickname sends jealousy clawing out of its frame. "And for your career. The value of your work…" There are many things he could say about the value of her work in relation to my interest in it. It's one reason I stay away from most contemporary artists. An offhand compliment from me can send an artist's esteem skyrocketing. This becomes a problem if my interest is taken as an endorsement. "He sees the value in it," Robert says. The acoustics of the space send his voice out to the gallery as if he were standing next to me. "I think he loves the new piece, too. He couldn't stop looking at it."

Another pause, this one shorter. "See you in five."

He comes back out with a cascading click of beads. "The artist lives nearby. She'll be here shortly. Her name is Daphne."

"Daphne." A shallow nod.

The piece isn't what I thought it would be. That's why I can't stop staring at it. I thought she'd paint what she saw from her place on the beach. But then—this is what she saw from her place on the beach. A man out in the water. I flatten my emotions into frames. Turn them facedown. Close the door.

I take stock of the rest of my body. No outward signs that I'm feeling anything. No tension in my shoulders. No expression but mild interest. It's essential this doesn't get away from me.

It's essential nothing gets away from me.

"Take your coat?" Robert asks.

"Sure."

I hand it off to him largely to give him something to do. He hangs it on a hook behind the counter and busies himself with his ledger. Flips pages back and forth. A fan circles overhead, moving warm air over the back of my neck. He kept it dim in here tonight so the pieces stand out under their picture lights. These fucking paintings. Sea salt and a stiff breeze. I can feel the icy pull of the current on my fingertips. Night air crackles in my lungs. I reach equilibrium when I resurface in cold like that. Frozen inside and out.

A door in the back opens. Robert abandons the ledger and pokes his head behind the beaded curtain. A murmured question from Daphne. "Out here," he says. "No, you're good."

All the work I've done to keep my emotions in check, and the physical responses won't stop. Goose bumps run up my arms. My lungs feel oversized. My heartbeat is naturally low, but it ticks up regardless.

Daphne steps into the room. She's partially hidden behind Robert. They have a quick, quiet conversation. I hear *buyer* and I hear *commission* and I hear *any other pieces, if*—

"All right." Her voice lifts, clear like an open window after several days in the dark. "I'll text you when it's time to lock up."

He's getting his coat. Putting it on. "I'm getting a coffee. Place on the corner."

"See you in a little bit."

My painter steps into the main gallery as he leaves. Robert has to pull hard on the door and it closes with a bang. "Hello." A few more steps. Quick. Light. Not particularly timid, but not rushing, either. "I'm Daphne, and I—"

I can't wait any longer to turn.

Daphne is caught, half bathed by the yellow tint of one of the picture lights and half in the silk shadow of the rest of the gallery. Surprise chases across her eyes. The gold flecks stand out like embers floating up from a fire. A moment of denial. It can't be. A half-step closer to confirm. I'm not wearing a wetsuit this time. Her eyebrows draw together in dismay. She tracks something behind me—Robert, crossing in front of the gallery. I can tell when he's gone, because her eyes come back to mine with a shadow of fear.

I've never seen anything this beautiful. The best work of the old masters never hurt like this. My lungs burn, holding a breath that isn't there. My heart flattens itself along the back wall of my body, palms against wood, beating hard. Too valuable to be out here like this. She's too priceless. Too vulnerable.

And she's in here with me.

Daphne Morelli is a thousand delicate details. I thought the impression might have less impact here in the gallery. I was fucking wrong. It's all there, in her eyes, on her face. She's afraid. Out of her depth in a way she didn't expect. Quick breaths. Shallow. Every movement changes the pattern of shadows over her dress.

I wrestle my own responses aside. Shove them away. Try the door.

There. Locked away. I can breathe.

My painter steels herself with one last breath. Perfect lips turn down at the corners.

"You." A one-word accusation. "You lied to me." She's flushed with anger and surprise, a soft pink high on her cheekbones. This is a taste of what I could get from her. This is the surface, and there is so much more below. The most important thing is to keep her here. Daphne's weight is on the balls of her feet, like a bird waiting to take flight. And yet—she is still leaning toward me, more than she is leaning away.

"I didn't lie."

"You lied by omission. You didn't tell me who you were."

She didn't ask. We talked about surfing. We talked about paintings.

"No. I didn't."

Daphne blinks. Not expecting honesty, then. "Would you have told me if I asked?"

This is the crucial moment, the crucial answer. The scent of her is so light. So pure.

"Yes. But it would have been a mistake."

Her fear edges toward curiosity. "How so?"

"You didn't want names, otherwise you would have given me yours. Beyond that, it would have influenced the work. Boxed you in. I wanted you to have artistic freedom."

There—the magic word. Daphne's chin lifts. She steps further into the light. Her eyes are so dark, but so alive—they remind me of the way she paints the deep ocean. A sense of movement. A dark intelligence. Secrets, secrets—

I keep my hands in my pockets. "Show me around."

"I should text Robert and tell him we're done

here."

I should.

The way Daphne said it was very nearly a question. She managed to keep it from becoming one at the last moment, but it was enough. There is usually someone in Daphne's life who tells her what to do. Who has, no doubt, told her what to do in situations like this one. At the very least they've warned her away.

Except she can't bring herself to leave. *I should* leaves space for possibility. It begs for an answer. A proposition more compelling than a tour of the gallery. This place didn't earn a mention in our conversation at the beach. With her, I'll need to be much more specific. Adrenaline drips into my consciousness. Understanding a person involves trial and error, and in Daphne's case, extreme care.

She's given me enough to go on.

"Show me your art." This tone, a confident demand, has an effect on Daphne. A glimmer catches the gold in her eyes. She won't be able to resist my authority. She wants me to see. "Show me what you painted for me."

Chapter Six

Daphne

I SHOULD NEVER have fallen for him at the beach. Obviously. I've never felt so foolish in my life. I wanted him to ask for my number. I hoped for that. I was prepared to give it to him, and now look.

He's not who I thought he was at all.

He's the Collector, and he came here for me.

Robert also made it clear that he's powerful, and rich. I don't like rich guys. My brother is the only one I can stand. My father and everyone like him is a privileged asshole, and none of them care about art beyond having a designer choose pieces they can show off at parties. I love parties, but I've never liked meeting the men there. The Collector is definitely one of them.

I just—how? How is it him? I thought the Collector would be old and filmy and boring.

This man is not boring. He's the least boring person I've ever seen. The tall, beautiful body I saw in a wetsuit is in a real suit now. Charcoal. A white shirt underneath. The color of the shirt looks calibrated to his skin somehow. The outfit on him makes my mouth water.

And then there's him. The strong shapes and lines weren't an illusion created by the wetsuit. They're all here, wrapped in what's probably virgin wool and thousand-dollar cotton. There's something refined about his features, but strong, too—I could see him staring out at me from a painting in the Met, except there's no roundness to his face. Very little softness. He's got eyes like I've never seen. Blue, but not like the Constantines. They're darker. Hinting at teal. I would have to be closer to see.

I want to be closer.

And I should get the hell out of here.

Everything he's said is perfectly reasonable, and that's why I should leave. It was the same way on the beach. I wanted to listen to him talk all night. I couldn't stop looking at him in his wetsuit. I wanted those things because I didn't know what he was.

Oh, this is bad. Leo would freak out if he knew I was doing this. Last week he made me take extra security to meet with another gallery owner. It was a whole thing involving a trip to his house because he thought the other gallery was somehow shadier than Motif. He was right, which I haven't told him, and I am definitely not going to tell him that I allowed myself to be left alone here. Honestly, he deserves it. He wouldn't tell me anything about the woman he has staying with him. Haley. Who was pretty and kind and a little bit cagey, if you ask me. She was so nervous. So surprised by me.

The world has gotten me back. I'm surprised by this man.

"I didn't paint it for you," I say finally. "I didn't know it was you."

His mouth lifts in a smile and an alarm goes off in my head. Loud. Screaming. That smile makes me want to hear him laugh. He didn't laugh on the beach. He took me seriously. No one takes me that seriously. "You did. But we can pretend it wasn't a commission, if you'd like."

Oh, god. I told him about that, too. I was so excited I couldn't shut up about it. I called it the most important painting of my life. He stands next to my pieces, not looking at them.

He only has eyes for me.

"I'll show you the gallery first." Because if I start talking about that damn painting now, I might start laughing and never stop. Or start crying and never stop. "You can come this way."

He's there in three quick strides. Close, but not too close. He could reach me if he wanted, but he doesn't. *Closer*, a voice whispers in the back of my mind. I want him closer. I don't know why. I shouldn't, shouldn't, shouldn't. I feel like I'm breathing champagne. Bubbly and cool. I pat my phone in my pocket. Robert is a text away. Same goes with the security team.

The Collector's eyes flick down when I do it. I'm regretting the long sleeves now. I'm overheating in this dress. Overheating in the force of his gaze. I stare back into it and pretend I'm at a family dinner. Or at one of the fundraisers. Or at Christmas. At those events, I'm Daphne Morelli, and Daphne Morelli doesn't let everything show on her face.

Some things, because I'm a person and not a statue.

Not everything.

"What are you looking at?" His voice is beautiful and level and casual, but this does not feel casual. I'm staring.

"I'm trying to decide what color your eyes are." It feels bold to admit it. "It's hard to tell when there's no natural light."

"What would you use if you painted them?"

"I wouldn't." This gets another smile out of

him. Victory. I really shouldn't be thinking of his smiles in those terms, but I can't turn off the firefly glow of pleasure near my heart. "I would start with gray," I admit. "But I'd be forced to layer in blue and green. If I painted your eyes. Was it a joke?"

He goes back to watching me. Jesus. No one has ever watched me with an intensity like this before. Like every breath I take is a monumental change. "Was what a joke?"

"The commission. Did you even want a painting?" Or did he want to get me alone on the beach? I was the one who thought of it as a commission. He wrote down a place and a time, and I jumped in headfirst.

"I didn't want a painting." My heart tears like cheap canvas. "I wanted your painting. I had to see what you would make of my beach."

The ripped canvas knits itself back together. The cold of that night comes back to me. In my fingertips. Beneath my shoes. But it's an exhilarating cold.

"My name is Daphne."

"Emerson." He holds out his hand to me to shake. I've touched him before. He helped me up from my chair that night. Touching him now seems more dangerous. I stick my hand out anyway and put it in his. He hasn't been swimming, so his skin is warm and dry and he squeezes my hand for exactly the right amount of time. Not a second more. It's such a perfect handshake that I don't want to let go when it's over.

I clear my throat and face the first piece down from mine.

"This is from a local artist. The theme has to do with the passage of time in the city, and for her medium…" Off and away. I give these little speeches about paintings whenever someone asks. Robert likes for me to be prepared when someone does come in, so most times I practice them by myself. Sometimes over the phone to Eva. She always pretends to be in the gallery with me, asking ridiculous questions about the art. But she hasn't called this week. Radio silence from my sister.

Emerson listens to every word I say. He doesn't ask many questions. Once he asks, "Does the artist have other work?" Another time he says, "Any other showings?" Otherwise he says nothing, letting me lead him around like this is anything to him. I keep waiting for his reaction. Bracing myself for when he responds to a painting that's not mine.

We stop in front of the display wall. There are

a couple more left before mine. "Here we have the pride of Motif Gallery. It's a Peter Clay original."

Robert wants me to sell paintings. I get it. What's good for the gallery is good for me. And it's a good painting, in a technical sense.

A young woman looks out at me from the frame. She's nude, her arm placed carefully over her breasts, and she's crying.

People love this painting. They can't stop talking about it. When we get customers here, they all have questions about Peter's work. Any moment now, Emerson will comment on how lucky we are to have a piece like this. Or he'll talk about Peter's talent as an artist. He'll say something. I'll stand here and nod along. That's my job. This private showing with this rich, gorgeous man is my job. I look at the woman in the painting instead.

Any second.

Emerson crosses his arms in front of him. I don't want to see his face, so I only get a hint of the motion out of the corner of my eye.

The silence continues.

Radiators kick on at the back of the gallery. A car passes by on the street outside. The tear on the girl's face stays where it is with a realistic glisten.

Great. He's completely taken with this painting, like all the rest of them. The rest of the visitors to the gallery. Everyone who ever came to an exhibition when I was in college. Emerson, the famous Collector, is so head over heels that he's speechless.

More silence.

The radiators go off. Impatience taps at my ribs. Irritation. I'm not going to stand here all night so he can get his thoughts about Peter Clay in order. I have other things to do. I could watch one of my shows. I could paint. I could text Eva and ask to come over. Anything but this.

I turn my head to tell him so, and the snappy comment I was going to make dives under the floorboards.

He hasn't been looking at the painting.

He's been watching me.

For longer than I realized. Much longer. He's settled into it. Emerson's eyes hold mine while shivers race down the ridges of my spine. They narrow slightly as it happens. Taking me in. Men have looked at me before, but no one has ever seen me. Not like this. And everything in him—it feels like a response, somehow. He hasn't moved away but he hasn't moved in, either. It's watchful, as if…

As if I'm not myself. As if I'm someone he

should take care around. It's nothing like the way people are with my brothers, Leo especially. For one thing, Emerson isn't afraid.

"You don't like Peter Clay's work."

"It's—" Our conversation from the beach tumbles through my head. "The art and the artist can't be separated."

Emerson glances back at the painting. No reaction. He'd probably put more emotion into picking bread at the grocery store. And then he's crossing the last few feet to the opposite wall. Two more paintings. One.

And then we're in front of mine.

I know I shouldn't care. I shouldn't watch him approach. It's that I have to know. I have to see for myself what he thinks of my work.

The Collector pauses between the two canvases, several feet back so we can see them both. Excitement and dread bubble in my veins. There's a strange pressure that makes me breathe deeper. And the heat—my cheeks, my hands, the back of my neck. I'm embarrassed to have painted this. I'm embarrassed that I stayed up all night to do it, thinking of how much the mysterious Collector might like it. The security people across the street were up, too. Lights on all night, all week. Almost like they knew someone was coming.

It's none of their business. It's my business, and I want answers.

"Why?" I round on him. "Why didn't you tell me who you were?"

He shrugs. "I'm no one. And I didn't want to influence the work."

"If you didn't want to influence my work, why did you leave me the address of that beach?"

Amusement glimmers in his eyes. "Because I own it."

No way. "You own a public beach?"

"A long stretch of it. That part is on loan to the city for twenty years."

"Why?"

He glances back at my painting and another hot flush tumbles down from my head to my toes. "I thought I shouldn't be the only person who got to see the sunset."

My humiliation softens. It's the kind of thing an artist would say. So much of the world is off-limits to people, and that means we can't paint it. We have to fight and scrabble and pay admission, and I don't think that's right. Emerson understands that.

A prickle of nervousness interrupts the warmth I feel. I wouldn't normally meet a patron that way. For one thing, I'm not a big enough name for that, so it's random people buying my work. For another…the address. The time. It's true that I went of my own free will, thinking I was visiting a public beach.

But.

Emerson is exactly the kind of person I should be afraid of. It doesn't matter how beautiful he looks in the partial illumination of the gallery, all perfection in an expensive suit. He's someone full of privilege, like my father. Wealthy, commanding, and ultimately a bully.

I can't have feelings for him. This is strictly an art collector and an artist. A transaction. Over as soon as the money changes hands. That's all it'll ever be.

CHAPTER SEVEN

Emerson

EVERYTHING ABOUT DAPHNE Morelli is mesmerizing.

Her art. Her body. The hummingbird breaths that make her chest rise and fall in her unassuming navy dress.

I have never been so invested in the oxygen exchange of another person. Not like this. My awareness of her supersedes every past focus. I would have sworn there was nothing more heightened than waiting for the sound of footsteps outside a locked door, but there is, and it's watching Daphne Morelli breathe. It's watching the light play in her huge, dark eyes. More intense by the minute. She goads all the emotions I keep far away. Goads them into becoming something real, something in motion. She's been standing so close, for so long, the scent of her in the air and her voice in my ears and her fluttering heartbeat. I swear I can hear it.

The only thing to do when confronted with

this much sensation is to walk away. Get back into the familiar exchange of a purchase. And leave, at the end. Leave and never come back. Stay detached. That's the way to stay alive. Keep your eyes on those slices of light at the door. They're a warning. Something more dangerous than you is coming.

She could wreck me, out in the world like this. Better to keep her where I have control.

But Daphne isn't something to acquire.

Not yet.

She's much more than a statue. I can't picture her in marble. She's too warm for that. Her emotions play across her face like shadows on a hillside. Humiliation and curiosity. Anger and fear. Understanding, when I say the bit about other people seeing the sunset, which has the benefit of being true. But then a wariness creeps into her eyes, and I can't stand it.

I can't shove this emotion, this want, away from me. It won't go. She's so near. So warm. So alive. The air between us feels like an insult. The fact that I'm not touching her is a grave mistake.

Her huge, dark eyes skip down over me, the glance involuntary, and when she looks back into my eyes—

Longing. Her face is filled with longing. I

recognize it from the photo in my report. Flushed cheeks and wide eyes and a set to her mouth that begs for something, anything, other than standing here like two pieces on a chessboard.

One step toward her, and Daphne freezes in place, a deer caught in headlights. Another step, and she's alive again, anticipating me. Responding. A flash of fear, but she doesn't run. She lets me back her into the far corner of the gallery. She lets me trap her there.

My shadow falls over her, but her eyes stay bright. Catchlights flicker like stars. She's breathing fast and sweet.

One of her hands comes up to the front of my jacket. A test, I think. To see what I'll do. I'd bet anything that Daphne Morelli isn't this cautious when she's at her canvas. It's the smallest connection between us. Slim fingers between the buttons. Not to pull me close. Not to push me away.

I want to pin her to the wall. That need surges through my veins, skipping out of bounds. But that would mean losing control. That would mean giving it up entirely.

I can't do that with Daphne.

She's more birdlike than ever, touching me like this. It's an opening move. An invitation, really. Her breath hitches. I press one palm flat against the wall to keep from looping it around her throat. Her eyes follow the movement, but she's quick about it, as if she thinks it's dangerous to look away from my face for more than a glance.

As if she doesn't want to look away.

Fuck me, I want to be touching her. More than this. Her knuckles burn a hole in my shirt, straight through to the skin. There are a thousand positions I'd like to see her body in, a thousand sounds I want her to make for me.

But.

For as much desire is in the air around her, as much sweet, innocent desire, she's also skittish. The way she flinched at the beach told me more than she wanted. My heartbeat slows. It beats harder to compensate. Like a tolling bell. My mind hurries through all the available options, all the ways I could touch her. No and no and no.

I put my hand over hers instead.

A short breath escapes her at the contact. Her fist closes tighter around the seam of my jacket. A moment of tension. The air is strung on a wire. It could snap any second. I feel like I'm having a heart attack. The wait is killing me, but I do wait, I do fucking wait. I am extraordinarily practiced at waiting.

Daphne's hand relaxes under mine. I feel the rest of her body go with it, leaning in a fraction of a degree. I brush my fingers over the back of her hand, her wrist, to the sleeve of her dress. Over her slim forearm, her elbow. Deliberate. I have never been so deliberate in my life. Her upper arm. Her shoulder. She holds herself still but she can't hide the trembling any more than a bird could stay in flight without beating its wings. I toy with dark curls on her navy dress, push them carefully out of the way, and then I touch her skin. My hand around the side of her neck, my thumb on her jawline.

"Oh," Daphne says, and the heat in her voice is permission to tip her head back—not far, just enough—and kiss her.

It's like being hit with an ocean swell. The inverse of a swell. She's not force and salt. She's sweetness. Warmth. But then—yes. A dark mystery, too. Depths. She opens her mouth like she's been starving for me. Her pulse goes wild under my palm. An invisible timer ticks down. Too much longer and I'll be lost in her, in the delicate lips and tongue and teeth. In the exploration of her, which could go on and on and on. If I had more time. If I could let go.

Can't—can't do that.

Not now. Not with her. The tip of her tongue darts out to meet mine and she tastes me back.

Enough. Enough. Enough.

I push us away from the wall with one hand and bring her along with the other. Back to the light. Back to her painting. The timer runs out. It hits zero and the only way I can bring myself to stop is to turn her around.

But I can't let go.

I keep her body against mine. Daphne can't resist this. She's gone weak in the knees and she leans into me like I'm a structural piece in her life and not a stranger who lured her to the beach. No doubt she can feel how hard I am, but she doesn't pull away. We could be a couple at an art gallery. If anyone walked by the window, that's all they would see. Me, holding her close, one arm across her chest. She hooks both hands onto that arm like she's not sure of her balance.

Focus. With my other hand I find one of her wrists and trace the same path to her elbow, to her arm, up to the side of her neck. She's so afraid, and she wants this so much. She lets out a little sigh when I touch her again in the same way. Same pressure, same place on her neck. Daphne's struggle for composure is so beautiful like this. With her face hidden, it's all movement. All touch.

"Tell me, little painter. Why did you choose that perspective?"

She swallows. I keep the pressure on her neck light and even, hardly moving. "Because." A long, slow breath. "Because I saw a man surfing. It was a new angle. I hadn't painted it before."

"What was your inspiration? Before you saw that man. Why paint the ocean?"

Back down her shoulder, down her arm. To her waist. She's shorter than she appeared in those photos. Daphne leans into this touch, too.

"I can't stop," she admits. It sounds like something she hasn't told anyone else. A secret she's been struggling to keep, perhaps. "At first it was some commentary about how the water hides things, and how it's never the same twice. How it's the last frontier and everything. Now it's more than that. It's in my head." Her fingers press against my arm like she's remembering the keys of a piano, and I want more of her. Want it so much that I take the risk of sliding my hand up and up until I meet the curve of her breast under her dress. "It's—" Daphne shivers. "It's all that ends up—"

"All that ends up where?"

"All that ends up on the canvas," she whispers.

Jesus, it's adorable. "It's a problem," she says in a clearer voice, "because people won't be interested in the same subject forever."

"I'll buy every piece." I mean it. I don't want any of them in anyone else's home. "I'd buy the artist."

"What?"

"Come back to my house with me. I'll show you my art collection. I'll make it worth the trip." I want her so much it hurts, and it's a long shot, I know it is. But there's a slim chance she could agree, and anyway, money is all I have to offer. It's the only way to have good things in the world. It's the only way to keep them safe. "I'd pay what you're worth."

Daphne jerks out of my hands and rounds on me, blinking like she's woken from a deep sleep and found herself in a nightmare. She puts her hand to the collar of her dress and grips it tight. Her hand is shaking. She's the one who's lost control now. Too late to get it back. Her face is shadowed again, her body backlit by the gallery lights. Her dress is a similar shade to the deep sea behind her.

"No." One step back, and then another. "I'm not selling you any more paintings. And I think you should leave."

She's already in flight. Daphne sweeps the beaded curtain aside, the sound in disarray, and they slap against the doorframe. I force myself not to go after her. I concentrate on the pools of gallery light and shadow. Corners of canvas and knots in the wood floor. A door slams.

And Daphne forgets.

She forgets that she's supposed to be living nearby, not upstairs, and her footfalls are heavy on the stairs at the side of the gallery.

They pause halfway up.

I can still taste her. Still feel her in my hands.

She'll be thinking of me. Is she frozen there on that step, her heart pounding? Listening with everything she has?

I make my footsteps purposefully loud on the way to the gallery counter, stopping only to scrawl a note on a stolen page from the pad and collect my coat. I don't hesitate on the way to the front door. I don't stop at the display wall with the Peter Clay piece. I don't stop for anything, because if I do, I'll lose control. I'll go to where Daphne Morelli is trembling on the staircase. I'll take what I want from her.

The lock on the door flips easily under my hand. The door opens without a fight. I'd half-hoped they wouldn't, but the gallery makes no effort to keep me inside. It lets me out into the night. A cold wind blows, rustling stray litter on the concrete.

I don't want to go. I don't want to leave Daphne Morelli behind. It's not sensible to leave something so precious all alone, where anyone could get to it. Walking away from the gallery feels wrong, like walking through water. Fuck me. It's even less sensible to get attached. Far more dangerous to feel anything about anyone. But I do. Light pollution hangs in the sky like an orange stripe, blocking out the stars.

I need to know more about her. I hate to leave her. Each thought goes into its own separate frame, all in a row, where I can see them. Where I can keep them in line.

Leaving is a foolish thing to do.

I won't be gone long.

CHAPTER EIGHT
Daphne

I T'S TOO BRIGHT in my room when I wake up. I don't think it counts as "waking up" if you feel like you haven't slept. I roll over in the bed and cover my face with the sheet. Too bright, and too early. White light like snow pours in the window and tries to get in through the sheet.

Obviously, I forgot to close the blinds last night. My face heats and I pull the sheet back down to breathe. He for sure heard me running up here, stomping up the stairs, and then stopping when I realized what I'd done. If he didn't know where I lived before, he does now. And after Robert followed his part of the security plan, which is to never tell anyone that I live upstairs.

Leave it to me to blow it.

I swipe my phone from the bedside table and peer at the screen. No new messages. None from Eva, or Leo, or even Sophie, who sometimes stops here when she wants a break from running wild all over the city. The quiet is weird. But it's what I wanted, right? Some space to be a grown adult. Though part of being a grown adult is knowing when you've made a mistake, and I have definitely made a mistake with Emerson.

It doesn't matter that nothing has ever felt as good as his hands on mine. As his mouth on mine. It was a mistake. A foolish, reckless mistake.

I know what Leo would say if I called to tell him what happened. He'd be worried, and he'd pretend not to be worried. I would try to keep things surface-level—*one of the gallery customers found out where I live.* Then he'd demand to know who it was, and how they found out. And I wouldn't name names, because...

Because I liked the way he tasted. I liked how warm he was, and how interested he was, and I wanted to see that particular blue-green shade of his eyes while he looked at me. Under no circumstances am I supposed to like those things, or invite them at all, but they happened, and I liked it.

On top of that, he scared the shit out of me.

And when people hurt me, when people scare me, when Leo finds out about it, he doesn't let it rest.

The security people have already been extra

visible this week. If I admit that a man came into the gallery and scared me—and then kissed me— they wouldn't stay across the street, they'd move into my living room.

The phone rings in my hand. It startles me so much I drop it and it hits me in the collarbone. "Ow," I scold, and then I pick it up and answer it.

"Hey, Daphne." It's Robert. "How are you?"

"Good. I'm good." I sit up and prop the pillows behind me. It feels weird to talk to Robert when I'm in bed, but at least when I'm sitting up I can pretend to be more professional. "Did you need something before my shift this afternoon?"

"Just—" He clears his throat. "How did the showing go last night? You guys had already headed out when I got back."

"It was fine."

"Yeah? What did he say about the pieces?"

Across the street, the windows of the security apartment reflect back my own uncovered windows. "He thought they were good."

Also, Robert, I told him I wouldn't sell him any more paintings. I told him he should leave. I told him that because, in addition to kissing me like no one's ever kissed me in all my life, he suggested he wanted to buy me.

The thought of saying all that makes me want

to crumple into a ball, pull the blankets back over my head, and die.

"He must have, judging by the note."

My palm goes slippery on my phone case. "What note?"

Robert laughs a little. "He left a note here on the counter. It says—*D.M.'s work is underpriced. Tell her I'm offering fifty thousand. Per painting.*"

A hundred thousand dollars for two paintings. Anger builds behind my shock. He's taunting me now, offering an amount that makes my refusal seem petty. He's going to sweep it aside with his money and pretend I never refused him.

"No, I don't think so." I steel myself for Robert's disappointment, because there's no way. There's no way I can accept this. No way I can sell to him and give Emerson the impression that I'm for sale. It's bad enough I let him touch me for so long. It's bad enough I let him kiss me. It's bad enough I wanted it, and he could tell. "I don't want to sell to him."

The silence goes on so long I pull the phone away from my ear to make sure we're still connected.

"Robert?"

"I'm here. Daphne…" The ledger rustles in the background. He's probably flipping the pages back and forth in one of his nervous habits. "It's your call, of course, but a sale of this size…"

"It won't end, that's the thing." I won't go into too much detail about what happened last night, with Robert least of all, but I have to say something. "He doesn't just want these two. He wants to buy all my paintings. That's too much."

"All of them? He wants to claim all your future work?"

"That's what it sounded like."

He whistles. "That would be—I mean, if this note is anything to go by, you wouldn't have to worry about anything."

When Robert says *anything*, he means money. I wouldn't have to worry about money. If Emerson is serious about buying even half of the pieces I plan to paint in the foreseeable future, it means a ton of money for me, and a huge commission to the gallery. Shame burns at the back of my throat. It feels bad to say no, but it feels worse that I fell for his lies. Emerson made me feel special, only to treat me like a prostitute. Like a person for sale. Why can't I get that through my head? Why can't I forget how good it felt to kiss him.

"I don't think that's true. I think I'd have quite a bit to worry about."

"You'd be set," he insists. "Even if he didn't want them all, your work would be so valuable, Daphne. People would be lining up for showings."

I can hear how much he wants this, and what I hate most of all is how conflicted I feel.

Emerson was an incredible kisser. He was also a liar. He didn't tell me who he was until he wanted something from me, and what he wanted turned out to be everything. He wanted to make a purchase of me.

And I'll never admit that when he said it, with his body against mine, something went hot and liquid between my thighs. Before my brain snapped back to being offended, I liked it. I liked the way it sounded when he said it. Pure possession. That's what it was. No two ways about it.

"Just think about it." Robert manages to say this casually, which has to be tough for him. "Don't decide anything today. It was a big night. Take some time, okay?"

"Okay." Mainly, I want this conversation to end. "I'll think about it. I'll see you later on."

I hang up and roll facedown into the pillows.

This is not how I imagined it would go when someone finally discovered my work, if they ever did.

There's a knock at the door. I bet anything it's Robert, feeling weird about the conversation. "One minute," I say into the pillow. It's not loud enough for whoever it is to hear me. It's more of a personal commitment to getting out of bed. I do, and throw on a hoodie and leggings. I catch a glimpse of myself in the mirror on the way past the bathroom. Good thing, too, because my hair is a mess. A bun on the top of my head is an improvement. "Coming," I call toward the door.

No one answers.

I slide the privacy cover on the peephole out of the way and look out.

Nobody in the hall, either. Some canvases I have stored out there. A package, maybe. I usually have things delivered to the gallery, but it's not out of the question.

I pat my hair one last time and flip the lock. Open the door.

There's no package waiting on the navy blue doormat.

There is a single, white orchid.

Goose bumps paint themselves from the top of my head to the base of my spine. It's all I can do to pick my head up and look down the hall to make sure there's no one there. My heart jumps into my throat and bangs around. The hall is empty. I take two shaky steps toward the stairs and look down. They're empty, too.

But someone was here.

Someone left me a white orchid.

It was him. I know it was him. There's only one person who would have any reason to leave me a flower, and it's Emerson, and...

He knows. He knows where I live. He was standing down in the gallery when I came up.

I followed you, this flower says.

I stand over it on the doormat, my hands shaking. If I pick it up, does that mean I'm accepting what happened last night? That makes me want to crush it in my fist, take it down to the sidewalk, and throw it to the concrete.

A distant buzz comes from inside the apartment.

My phone.

I swipe the orchid from the doormat and rush in. Slam the door. Lock it tight. It's a pure, delicate flower. White as snow. Flawless. It feels so fragile in my hand. There's a warmth to the stem. Like he was holding it in his big palm.

The phone's still ringing when I get to the bed. Eva's name is on the screen. "Hi." I sink down on the side of my bed, trying not to sound out of breath. "Why are you calling so early?"

And then I can't help it. I bend my head to the petals and take a deep breath in. Soft petals. Delicate. Pure. I'm hoping for a trace of him, for the fresh-air scent of him. I want it more than I can say.

I want him more than I should ever want a rich asshole who wants to buy me.

"Hey, Daph." Eva sounds tired. More than tired—exhausted. Afraid, almost. My stomach drops. All those days she didn't text feel different now. And the way the security apartment was all lit up, all week. "Are you at home?"

"Yeah, of course I am. It's barely daylight." I force a laugh. "Are you at home?"

"No, actually. I'm at the hospital. New York-Presbyterian."

"Are you serious?" Blood rushes out of my face. It was hot a few seconds ago, but now my cheekbones feel frozen.

"Listen, everything's all right. I should have started with—it's fine. Everyone is going to be fine. I wanted to call and let you know."

"What's happening?" I try to sound as cool and collected as possible, but not knowing is terrible. "Was there an accident?"

I can't bring myself to ask about one person or another. Our family is too big. There are too many chances for something to go wrong.

"There wasn't an accident." Eva takes a deep breath, and I can't understand why she's having to steel herself if everything is going to be so, so fine. "I'm here because Leo is here."

Panic sets in. This is why she's trying to be so gentle about this. "For what?"

"He's going to be fine," she says. "That's the thing I need you to know. They patched him up, and he's going home tomorrow. Okay? I would have told you earlier, but he didn't want you to worry."

"Tell me what happened."

"He got shot, Daph." All the air squeezes out of my lungs. Eva keeps talking, but the words bounce off me and slide down to the floor. Something crumples in my hand. It's the orchid. My nails have bitten through the soft petals. The flower's ruined now.

CHAPTER NINE

Emerson

A S IT HAPPENS, a man can't have iron-willed control over everything in his life. Most things, but not everything. I'm willing to admit to myself that Daphne Morelli might be the exception to the many rules I have about emotions and their place in a man's mind.

I intended to leave several days between the showing and my first visit. Untenable, staying away that long. I didn't want her to wonder if I'd forgotten. Or worse, think that the kiss in the gallery was nothing to me.

It was not nothing.

It clarified an error I'd made in my thinking. Somehow, because I'm a fucking fool, I thought it was simple. I wanted to witness the transfer of emotion from her body to canvas. I haven't stopped wanting that. But I want something more, something that has less to do with art and more to do with the woman herself. Now that I've had my hands on her, all the things I want run riot around my head.

I want to see her fear and her desire and her darkness on her. Not in a representation. On her skin. On her face. Between her legs. I want to let my feelings for her loose on her. Scrawl them on her skin. It's a visceral want. It makes my hair stand on end and my flesh hot and my heart pound.

I want those things, and I'll take them. Take her. I've fucked beautiful women before. It's easy enough, with money like mine. My encounters have been like visiting a museum. All the artifacts stay behind when you're finished with them.

Daphne isn't like that. She's the first piece I've wanted to acquire. Needed to acquire. It's not enough for her to stay in her shitty apartment, making art where I can't see her. She belongs with me.

Inside my house, preferably. Behind several locked doors. Where nothing and no one else can get to her. Touch her. Ruin her.

It will have to be taken in steps. I saw her face when she was looking at me. Sheer longing. And a complicated fear. A simple fear might have driven her to run away when she discovered my presence, but the fact that she didn't means there's much more to be discovered. Coaxed out of her word by word, if that's what it takes. Touch by touch. Pain by pain.

The waiting would make me burst out of my skin if I hadn't started already. The lock on the alley door was shamefully easy to pick. Not a deadbolt in sight. I left the flower on her doormat and saw the light from the thin gap under her door. I knocked to guarantee she'd find it before it wilted. I heard her inside. Heard her voice. Speaking to someone who wasn't me, and fuck, I wanted to stay. Pick the lock that kept her from me. But I was patient, and as sensible as a person can be when his blood is on fire. I didn't even wait at the bottom of the stairs to hear her discovery.

I made other plans instead. Setting up this meeting, for instance. It's taken some time to get things where I want them. Impatience rises again, and I force it back down. Pick up the pace.

The flower had at least one effect. Daphne agreed to sell me the paintings through Robert at the gallery.

The rush of all these emotions can be managed by paying attention to other things. On the way down the block, I watch fine snowflakes spiral to wet concrete. Some of them land on the curved necks of the faux-antique street lamps in this neighborhood. It calms my racing heart, but it does nothing to put Daphne out of my mind. She'd be beautiful, too, with her body bent over my bed and my hand on the nape of her neck. There's a bitter wind this evening, but I'm walking nonetheless. My driver will meet me at the art dealer's. Logan is one of the good ones. He doesn't bother to ask questions, which is his second-best feature.

I go up the steps in front of the dealer's, which was once two separate brownstones that have been gutted and combined. The door opens as soon as I reach the top. A man in a dark suit with a red tie ushers me in. The foyer is under-stated, dark wood and neutrals. A solemn quiet rests over the space. Harder to achieve, in a city as big as this one, but well within reach of the man who owns the dealership.

"Mr. Leblanc. Good afternoon. Your coat?"

"Fine. Thank you."

He's deft with the coat, folding it over his arm like a servant from a period film. "Mr. Wynn is waiting in the back room. If there's anything I can get—"

I wave him off and head for the back. I've bought plenty of pieces from Michael Wynn over the years. Sold a few, too. I come here for expensive pieces and for appraisals. Wynn has an eye for authenticity that can't be fooled, and he's made this place one of the most secure when it comes to the art. We've made enough deals together that I know about the work that went into the renovations. No hollow drywall for Michael Wynn. The walls are fireproof, bullet-proof—if anything happens to a piece in here, it won't be for lack of trying.

Michael leans over a desk in a room that could easily be a den or an office. A sofa and an armchair face a fireplace, and in another corner is a wingback. Michael's desk is on the left side. Two doors in the back are shut tight. He writes something in broad strokes. Finishes with a line underneath. Then straightens up, face brightening. "Emerson. How was the trip in?"

"Uneventful. Anything new?"

"A few pieces out of Europe. I held them for you."

"Value?"

"Between a million and five," he says. "One in particular might be of interest."

"I'll take a look. I'm more concerned with the other piece."

"It arrived last night." Michael buttons his jacket, his expression slipping easily into seriousness. "Three armed couriers. Six separate signatures to confirm delivery, if you can believe it. Room two."

He leads the way into the second door in the back. Michael stops at a shelf and hands me a pair of gloves. He puts on his own, then steps to a wide table. The painting itself has been wrapped for delivery, and Michael lifts it up and takes off the covering layer by layer. When he's done he props the framed canvas in the center of the table.

"*Where the Ocean Meets Sky*. A mesmerizing piece that speaks to the solitude of man." Michael unveils the painting with reverence. "And authentic. The original, of course."

So it is.

He steps back and lets me examine the work. The signature in the lower right is correct. It's the first thing I check, but as with any major purchase, I look at the piece as a whole. A vast ocean creeps away from the edges of the canvas and surges upward at the three-quarter mark. It's dark water against a bruise-colored sea. I have the impression the water might eat the sky alive.

Lehmann did have an eye for color and light, like Daphne said. The work is good. I can recognize that while feeling nothing for it. No distant pain, no uptick in my pulse. This is the kind of piece I would sell at a profit and never think of again. But Daphne's thought of it often. There was real disgust in her tone when she spoke about it.

Daphne tried to cover it up, how much she hates this painting, and the dead man who painted it. But she couldn't. Her voice shook. Her mouth went tight. And when she laughed...

Pain.

I want to know why it hurts her. There's more than what she would admit on the beach. An experience from her life I have yet to uncover. She gave me a hint of it when she flinched away from my hand, but I want more than hints and allusions. I want to know who, and how. Research purposes. I can't know her without knowing those details. She might think of them as tiny brushstrokes, but they are wide swaths in the person she is. I think, though I have no proof yet, that they are keeping her from what she might become if I have my way with her.

A step forward gives me a closer view of the individual strokes. I have come across this artist's work before. It would be impossible not to. I recognize the way the brush makes contact with the canvas. Michael waits, hovering off to one side. I'm sure this is the original. Still, I start again at the left side of the piece and work my way across.

There are no signs it's been forged. The brushstrokes are correct. So is the layering of the paint itself. No bristles have been left behind. It's a perfect example of Lehmann's characteristic attention to light. There isn't much of it in a scene like this one, where the sun has only begun to rise, but he uses it to maximum effect.

This is the painting Daphne hates.

I take a step back and nod at Michael.

"I agree," he says. He'd have said so already if he didn't, but he's not one to rush the process. Michael comes to stand beside me.

I take out my phone. "Same account as usual?"

"Yes." Michael takes out his own phone and glances down at the screen while I tap in the amount and the authorization. I choose his account number from a list. A transfer of this size means I have to click several more checkmarks on the screen, but the process will be instant once I get to the last one.

Michael's phone vibrates in his hand. He double-checks the confirmation, then drops it into his pocket and puts out his hand to shake. Two million dollars, my account to his.

"I'll have it delivered." He's already reaching for the wrapping on the table.

"That won't be necessary. I'll carry it."

"Carry it?" His eyebrows go up. "It's no trouble, Emerson."

"Like this." I take off the gloves and drop them to the table, then pick up the piece in my hands. All the weight comes from the frame. The canvas itself is very light. Not a large painting to begin with. "If you could get the door." Michael can get the door, and he does, discarding his own gloves on the way. They'll be washed to within an inch of their lives before he uses them again. "Thank you."

"Of course."

He stays by my side all the way to the foyer. He's not often uneasy, but I can feel him wondering why in the hell I would carry a painting worth two million dollars in my bare hands this way. Michael will think it's the act of a man who's not thinking clearly.

There's weather outside. Snow. Freezing rain. Wind. Any number of people are out there. Too much space. It's gratuitous, really, how many unpredictabilities exist in the city. People lie to themselves all the time about it. They imagine that society keeps things in check, that our systems of roads and stoplights and policemen mean safety, but they don't. Of course they don't. I follow a pattern in the frosted glass next to the door. Watch the glare from the street lamp try to fight its way through to the wood frame. Clean and polished. My heart has begun to fight against the idea of stepping out into the afternoon. Sweat under my collar. Let Michael make his own assumptions.

He brings me my coat, and I prop the painting on a mahogany table near the entry. Do up the buttons.

"The other piece," he says.

"Later. Next week, if there's no hurry." If there's no one else he wants to sell it to.

"None at all," Michael answers. "I'll hear from you?"

"We'll schedule tomorrow." I pick up the Lehmann again. Something in my chest lifts. But it's not about the art itself. It could never be about this painting, now that I know Daphne hates it. I'm anticipating something else entirely. Michael's assistant comes in from a side room and stands at the door.

"Oh—one more thing." Michael looks relieved. He thinks I'll decide to have the piece delivered or let his assistant carry it. "Do you have a can of spray paint?"

CHAPTER TEN

Daphne

I WISH I didn't have to be at this family dinner.

Seven o'clock sharp. In the dining room. At my parents' house. It sounds like a game of Clue, but there's no mystery to be solved here. Not in this room, anyway. There are plenty of questions to be answered and I feel hot and vaguely sick with not knowing.

Angry, too.

The rest of us have been here since ten to seven. Sophia leaned over and told me about a club she went to until our mother sat down a minute later. Lucian and Tiernan sit nearest my father's empty chair, neither of them saying anything until Sophia mentions the office. "The office, Lucian," she says, and he raises his eyebrows and pretends to be shocked that she cares.

"You wouldn't believe the meetings," he says. "There's room, you know. If you wanted to do something worthwhile with your time."

Sophia makes a face at him. "Like what?"

"The mailroom would be a good fit."

She dismisses this with a wave. She's the ulti-mate socialite. A different tabloid every weekend. "I'm not interested in the family business."

"What are you interested in, sister mine? Let's see." He pretends to tick things off on his fingers. "Smoke-filled clubs. D-list actors. Starting fires. Have I covered all the bases?"

I send an apologetic glance her way.

She rolls her eyes. "Why don't you tell us what you've been doing lately, Lucian? You've missed lots of dinners this year. Aren't you supposed to be in charge of everything?"

"I'm here now. That's what counts."

My father comes in at seven sharp, stepping around the staff who are serving the soup course. It's what the chef calls rustic tomato, which means there are crushed tomatoes in it. My bowl comes down in front of me, china meeting hardwood with a dull click. I stare down at five fat croutons and a sprinkle of green oregano on the red surface. Leo hates this soup. I've watched him eat it a million times. You'd never know he hates it. He never gives it away.

One look around the table and my father's face darkens. "Where is my son?"

"Lurking around London, I'd imagine." Sometimes it's hard to tell if Lucian is being deadpan or an asshole. I like it best when he turns it on our father. I don't like much of anything tonight. Obviously, our brother Carter is not here. He's the smartest one, both in terms of grades in school and getting away from Bishop's Landing. He only comes home for special occasions, and sometimes he skips those, too. I wonder how he learned not to care. Or maybe he doesn't feel the same pressure. Most times, it's an obligation to be here, but easier than the consequences. My father's anger. My mother's disappointment. Path of least resistance.

Silver clinks against china. One of the servers refills Sophia's water glass. I could tip my bowl over onto the white linen tablecloth in a big, dramatic spill. Tomato and crouton everywhere. It would break the tension. Explode it, probably. I don't do it. I put the spoon into the crushed tomato and take a bite.

"Leo." My father's eyes tick down the table and meet mine. "Did he have somewhere better to be?"

I make my eyes big and slightly blank. He's watching me, but he's not necessarily asking me. The question could be for the room at large. I hope I look like I don't know. I hope he doesn't keep asking. Lucian looks across the table at Tiernan, who eats his own soup in silence.

This wouldn't be happening at all, if it weren't for everything else. That's how life is, right? Everything depends on the past. And in the recent past, my brother got shot by a Constantine bulldog in his own house. He spent a week in the hospital afterward. I saw him the other day, and he pretended to be fine. I know he was pretending because when I hugged him, the breath went out of him. I didn't hug him hard enough to make that happen.

Dying, I want to spit at my father. He's probably dying, or maybe even dead. Things like that happen, you know. Things take a turn. Your brother goes home from the hospital and days later he's burning with a fever that could kill him. That's all Eva would tell me. She won't tell me anything else.

I panicked, after I got that first phone call from her. I called Robert back and told him I'd sell the paintings to Emerson. The two things felt connected somehow. Like maybe, if I sold the paintings, he'd leave me alone and things would be better.

I don't plan on touching his money. It feels

fake in my account. Strange.

"Oh, Eva called earlier," my mother says from my right side. And what? Did Eva tell her the truth? Her expression is as placid as it always is. I don't know how she can stand it. Waiting around for my father to snap. He always does, eventually.

Fear skitters over the backs of my arms. I swallow it with another crushed tomato. There's nothing to be afraid of now. It would be great if my body would remember that. Usually, I don't have trouble. Usually I sit through dinner with a smile on my face and plenty to say about the weather. Usually Leo is here, and Eva, and there's nothing much for me to say anyway. I stay quiet. I stay invisible. It's a strategy that works, except for the times it didn't. But all that was a long time ago. I'm not a child anymore.

"And what, Sarah?"

"One of her charities, I'm sure." This, from Lucian. I keep my expression very, very neutral. He's still eating tomato soup.

"That's what she said." My mother waves her spoon above her bowl. "A donation of some sort. An endowment."

Dad doesn't buy this. "What would Leo have to do with that?"

Lucian laughs. "He's a whore for recognition.

Probably made the donation himself."

My mother covers her mouth with her hand. "Lucian."

"I'm sorry." He doesn't look sorry. "Maybe it's the tax deductions he likes the best."

It's easy to be irritated with Lucian. Nothing gets to him. Nothing bothers him. Rattles him. Makes him any less cocky, or mean. And now he's openly being an asshole about Leo at dinner for no reason. My fist tightens around my soup spoon. I don't know what I plan to do with it. Hurl a crushed tomato in his face? It would be satisfying. It would also cause a scene.

"What about you, Sophie?" My mother poses the question like we're all sharing things about our lives. Casually, like I'm sure other families do. "How's the contract with Tommy going?"

Only my mother calls world-famous designers by their first name. My sister swirls her spoon in her soup, which is still completely full. Her tone is flat. "Super great."

My father's frown deepens.

"That's lovely," my mother says, but her attention is on the server she's summoned from the side of the room. *More wine.* She may not be a perfect parent, but she's always been a perfect hostess.

Sophia is two years older than me, but smarter and more mature than me by far. I don't understand half of what she talks about. What I do know is that sometimes she comes to my apartment above Motif late at night, sparkling drunk and tired enough to sleep on my couch. She won't tell me where she goes or what she's doing, but she'll tell me endless gossip about the artists she sees in the clubs or at the bars or wherever she's been. We have coffee. We eat brunch. And then she puts on dark glasses and goes.

"And Daphne sold some paintings," she says, grinning at me.

I raise my eyebrows at her. Why? Why would she do that? I narrowly avoided my dad's attention, and now look.

"I did." I put on a big smile. "A few of my pieces at the gallery." I never should have told her about this. Clearly.

"That place," my father says, "is an embarrassment." He's definitely looking at me now. This is for me. Next to him, Lucian checks his phone under the table and frowns. Did Eva tell him what was going on? If she did, does he know more than I do? We're in the same room, and I can't ask him. Even if I do, I probably won't get answers. Another flare of anger burns me up. Embarrassment rings in my ears. "You should know better than to associate yourself with a place like that."

I move my spoon in a slow circle through the soup. "I don't know, Dad. They put up my painting for me, and it sold. That's how I'll get recognized as an artist."

"By living in a hovel?" His face is getting red, which is not a good sign. "Stop pretending, Daphne. Insisting on that place is childish. If you want to waste your time on playacting an artist, I don't care, but you don't have to slight this family to do it."

I'm pretty sure my ears have burst into flame. "I don't think it's a slight. My work is good."

"Not good enough."

"Good enough to sell. Good enough to get a commission."

I don't know what I'm thinking, talking back to him. It's never worth it. Always dangerous. Blood hums in my ears. My face has to be as red as this soup. It's bullshit, being here. Leo could die, and I'm angry at him. I'm worried sick about him. I should have skipped the dinner too. I could have made an excuse and painted until I was too tired to see straight. I'd have sorted all my feelings out on the canvas instead of swallowing them like curdled milk.

"Are you painting others?" Lucian asks.

I look at him, instead of my father. I can't tell whether he actually cares or whether he's saying something to end the silence. His dark eyes are narrowed. Bright. "For the gallery?"

A bored shrug, but that light doesn't leave his eyes. Lucian's always watching to see what makes people react. Or overreact. "For anyone."

"Maybe. Why?"

"Morelli Holdings could use some updated art in the meeting rooms."

"If you want art, use a dealer," my father snaps.

"Art dealers are thieves. Unless you know someone who's not." Lucian aims this at our father.

It's enough to turn the conversation away from me.

"Sophia," my mother says, and then there are two conversations happening. The crushed tomatoes are disgusting. I eat the entire bowl. My mother is still going on about an event she's planning. How Eva will be helping her, though time is getting a bit short, and people will notice if it's a disaster.

I sneak my phone out of the pocket of my dress and put it on my lap.

Daphne: I'm coming over after this

The main course comes. Braised chicken with a side of Brussels sprouts. I can't stand Brussels sprouts. They're never good. Tasteless, and the texture is always off.

Eva: Not tonight

Eva: Not good here

Not good at Leo's house. I have no idea whether that means he dies by morning or he's in a terrible mood, and I want to know. Maybe I should get over it and wait for the news like everyone else. But I can't force myself not to care. I can't get all these feelings in a decipherable order. What are you supposed to do when your favorite brother might die but no one wants to tell you anything? And all this to protect me. The way he always does. Except then what? What happens if it's actually as bad as Eva says it is?

I'm not just mad at him. I'm mad at myself. I let Leo protect me, I keep letting him do it, and now I feel like the world is falling out from underneath me. That's ridiculous. I should be able to stand on my own two feet. It's cowardice, what I'm doing.

And I hate it. I hate being treated like a child who has to be kept away from everything scary in the world.

It's too late for that anyway.

Eva: I'll text you in the morning, ok?
Daphne: OK

"Texting?" My mother frowns at me from her seat.

"No." I put my phone back in my pocket. "Thinking about my next painting."

When dinner is over, one of Leo's drivers is waiting at the front door. Thomas, his name is. "Any stops on the way home?"

"No. Thanks."

This SUV is different from the one Leo normally drives to dinner. This one is armored, which makes me want to throw up even more. It seems like the kind of thing he'd send in the event he died. More security, because if my brother actually died, I think there might be chaos. Maybe a real war between the families. Who knows. Anything could happen. I stare out the window all the way back to the city.

Thomas pulls to a stop in front of Motif and gets out to open my door. "I'll walk you up."

"I'm good," I tell him. "You can go."

He shakes his head. "I have orders to walk you up."

Another wash of uneasiness and anger, followed by sheer worry. I stick my key into the alley door and go in ahead of him. He stops me with a hand on my arm and insists on going up the stairs first. The armored car is one thing, but this? I want to pull the pillow over my head and wish for morning.

We stop on the doormat. "I could do a sweep of the apartment," Thomas offers, and I can tell he's technically been ordered to do a sweep of the apartment.

I roll my eyes. "That won't be necessary." I unlock the door with a flourish and step into the dark. "See? I'm home safe. You did your job. Good to go."

He glances behind me. I never leave lights on when I leave, so there's nothing to see but shadows. "Have a good night, Daphne."

"You too." When I flip the lock on the door, I make it as loud as possible. Hopefully Thomas hears. I'm safe behind a locked door, and nothing can happen to me. I won't be there for my brother because I must be sheltered. I'll be safe. That's what. Nothing but safe.

I step out of my heels, shrug off my coat, and pad into the kitchen. Dump my purse on the countertop. I need some water. Unshed tears sting my eyes. The taste of tomato soup won't get out of my mouth. I fill up the glass in the dark. Leo is allowed to be worried, and he's allowed to do something about it. I have to sit around and wait for Eva to tell me what's happening. It's not fair. And I know, I know. Life isn't fair. But I can be pissed about it in my own kitchen when I'm alone. Heartsick about it.

The water's not very cold, run from the tap, and it sloshes against the cup when I turn around.

Something's in the living room.

My heart jumps up into my throat. A person? No. It's square, and too short, like—Jesus, Daphne. I fumble for a light switch and turn on the light.

Like a painting.

Oh my god.

I creep closer like something might jump out from behind it, but nothing does. It's an expensive frame and an even more expensive painting.

The Lehmann piece I mentioned at the beach.

I would know this painting anywhere, and not because I want to—because it's famous. There are millions of postcards of this painting. Posters for people to hang in college dorms. Prints are sold everywhere.

This is the painting itself. This is the original. It's worth at least a million dollars. Maybe more.

It *was* worth that much.

Someone has painted a giant X across the canvas in black spray paint.

I always thought this piece was garbage, as much as the man who painted it. Now it's worthless trash.

CHAPTER ELEVEN

Emerson

FOR A FEW days, I leave her be.

I don't go to the city to watch her apartment. I don't call the gallery to find out if she has any new pieces. I don't send a man in the city to follow her family members.

Nothing.

I treated the sale of her paintings like a normal acquisition, and I have not pressed for more.

I stay away.

I do it to prove to myself that I can, but also to be strategic in the process of acquiring her. Scaring her off by moving in too fast will fuck the whole thing, so I don't. It's as painful as surfing in the frigid ocean. I'm out there every day in the salt and waves, my bones like ice. My hands take hours to warm up afterward. No one can say I haven't been out in the world. Fuck the snow and the breath-stealing cold. Wave after wave after wave.

Her apartment was like her. It was small and

sweet and she chose every piece of it. The knitted blanket on the back of the sofa. A bright blue teacup in the sink. Something you'd buy at a craft show. Pottery, not china, but the shape of it was perfect. I can see it cradled in her hands. I can see her laughing as she tries to take a sip from it. Her cheeks going pink with joy.

Daphne's bed.

She makes it in a haphazard way, the blankets pulled up but not smoothed. Daphne paints in her bedroom. It's all very quaint, for a Morelli. Her family has enough money to buy her a private studio, and she paints where she sleeps, her easel by the windows. Her paints wait in a case on the cushion of a window seat. An arched doorway leads back to the living room. No door to lock. Strange that she can sleep out in the open like that. A light burned outside her apartment while I was inside, cutting her front door from the frame.

I want so much to see it in daylight. But then—it's not really the apartment I want to see. It's her.

I push that feeling away. Deny it food. It won't shut up. I can ignore it for days at a time, but it's always there, howling. It's not enough that I have a plan in place. Not enough that I'm working toward getting her. One night I surf out past the point it's safe and roll off the board into open ocean. I can't drown the feelings, can't freeze them, can't keep them locked away.

I need to have her.

On the way back to shore, I do the more difficult task of letting the feelings become more than static images. More than framed prints. Not so much that I can't control them. Enough to stop my heart from pounding. It's awful. Being at the mercy of emotion is enough to make a person sick. To make them vulnerable. I can't have that.

The rest of the night is strange. Half of it I lie awake, watching the moonlight on the ocean, trying to wrestle those feelings back into frames. I try to hang them at even intervals on a blank gallery wall. When I do fall asleep, it's straight into dreams. Her face. Her mouth on mine.

"Hummingbird," I tell her in the dream.

"Yes," she says, and it's like she understands, but that would be impossible. A person like her could never. Fragments of light from behind a door.

"Don't look."

She doesn't answer. She is looking at me.

In the morning I call my brother from the car. All the naked tree branches have frosted. A thin layer of glass, wrapped around every twist in the wood. It seems impossible that buds will ever form again. I dial his number even though it's early.

It's not as early as the winter makes it look, but it's very firmly morning. It's the kind of light that could trick a person into sleeping in. Doesn't matter.

Sin never sleeps.

It's boring. That's what he says about sleep, as if he needs a 24/7 adrenaline rush to stay interested in life. And maybe he does. I think he avoids sleep for a different reason, though. Control. Scaling a mountain. Kayaking white water rapids. Crossing the desert with nothing but a backpack. They're a big *fuck you* to nature. Proof that he's not a victim to his surroundings. He'll dominate nature or die trying.

"Emerson," he says. He sounds surprised to hear from me. His voice inspires me to do nothing so much as hang up and never talk to him again, but I don't. The voice of a news anchor cuts off in the background. "How are you?"

"The same as always. I heard you were thinking of coming to town."

"Not thinking about it. I'll be there soon."

"Not here. You can't stay with me."

In the front, Logan sips coffee from a travel mug. I gave it to him for Christmas last year. It's supposed to keep drinks hot for nine days or something ridiculous like that. It must be all right, because he uses it all the time. Or else he's angling for a bonus. Just a joke. He doesn't have to angle. He's good at his job, or else he wouldn't work for me.

"Why?" He was watching TV. I haven't caught him about to jump out of a plane or off the side of a cliff. For once, it sounds as if my brother is inside like a normal person.

"Because I'm seeing someone."

"Like, what, dating?"

"I guess you could call it that."

Sin takes a beat. I wish I could forget what he looks like, what both my brothers look like, but I can see his expression now, clear as day. He has a way of furrowing his brow but not looking particularly bothered. "Is it serious?"

"Yes." It comes out quieter than I meant it to. More truthful. It's the truth, after all. The feelings I have are serious. If I can't ignore them, if I can't cut them out or force them away, they must be serious. They take up more room in my chest every minute. A need that verges on desperate, and a twin hate that she's not here.

"Did she move in?"

"Not yet."

My brother's silence goes on longer this time. He's got a ceiling fan, wherever he is. He's so quiet the noise cancellation on his phone doesn't pick it up.

"Emerson."

"What?"

"When you say dating, you meant…like a date, right?" Open suspicion edges Sin's tone.

"A restraining order would only complicate things."

"Emerson—where are you right now?"

The lamp turns on in Daphne's living room. Her shadow is diffuse behind the lace curtains. She's not close enough for her shape to be visible.

"I'm in the city," I tell him. "Don't come to my house."

I hang up on him before he can ask more tedious questions.

Daphne steps out into the alley, and then she's headed in my direction. She looks soft and rumpled, in lounge pants and a matching hoodie with the hood pulled up over her hair. Is she wearing—my god, she is. Bunny slippers. Daphne stops at the curb and checks both ways for traffic. There is none. With zero hesitation, she crosses the street. I'm so fucking glad to see her. It's the most bizarre thing. I didn't intend to talk to her today. She can't see me through the tinted windows. She knocks on my window regardless, as if she knows I'm here. I roll it down and there's nothing between us anymore.

"Surprise," I tell her.

Her dark eyes hold a mix of fear and flattery. "How long were you going to sit out here?"

"How did you know it was me?"

Daphne's teeth chatter a little. "This isn't really an area where glossy black SUVs like this sit and hang out."

I try not to notice her nipples through the hoodie. It's not made for warmth. It's made for fashion. For sitting inside houses that always have heat. She must be wearing next to nothing underneath. The hoodie reads *New York is always hopeful. –Dorothy Parker* in a typewriter font.

"Are you here because I sold you the paintings?"

"It doesn't hurt."

She pulls her hands into the sleeves of her hoodie. "This isn't really an area where people stand in the street and chat. It's not exactly safe."

"It's broad daylight." Close enough, anyway.

Daphne purses her lips. "It's still not...you

know. It's not the safest."

"You could get in and go with me."

Her eyes widen. "Where?"

"Back to the beach. I want to watch you paint it."

"The other pieces weren't enough?"

"No."

The corner of her mouth turns into a wry smile. "Is that all? Me, painting the beach?"

I'd like to watch you paint while you're naked. While you're crying. While I'm inside you. It would be the purest form of poetry. It would be like nothing you've ever done, nothing I've ever done, and I want it more than I have ever wanted anything.

"No."

"At least you're honest."

Perhaps. I haven't told Daphne anything, really. She knows nothing about me except what I want her to know. Real honesty might be admitting that I can hardly breathe when she's standing this close. That goose bumps run up and down my arms when I think of her alone. The dream I had last night. That would be honesty. What I said was a plain truth. I want more than to watch her paint. I want so much more.

It's painful to ask, when I could take her now. Daphne's petite. Small enough that if I opened the door, I could have her in my arms and in the back of the SUV with minimal effort. She could not outrun me. If I did, if I gave in to the electricity wiring my nerves, everything would come apart. It would take forever for her to trust me again. It would take so long to make her see.

"Come with me," I say. Her shoulders shake now with the cold. Daphne looks behind me, into the SUV, and glances up at Logan. This is a different calculation entirely than staying with me in the gallery. I know she made that call minute by minute. She was alive with her fear every second, and part of her loved it. I tasted it on her. Fear. Desire. Relief.

"I—" A door bursts open on the other side of my SUV, wood banging on brick, and Daphne jumps back from the SUV window. "What's going on?"

I search for an answer, but she's not asking me. Two men in suits come into the street. "Ms. Morelli," one of them says.

Daphne's hand goes to the pocket of her hoodie. She pulls out her phone and frowns at the screen, then shoves it away again. "Is something happening?"

"We need you to come this way."

"Guys." Daphne sighs, but she puts on a smile

anyway. "This is maybe not the way to do this. I'm in the middle of a conversation."

"We have orders," says the second one.

"What, is it because I'm outside?" Daphne's voice rises, but she doesn't lose control.

"No, Ms. Morelli. There's no problem with you being outside." The first one glances in my direction and doesn't seem to see me. "It's time to get ready to go. This way, please."

Another SUV pulls in front of the alley, and I know what I'm seeing now. I underestimated them. The Morellis. I should have known they wouldn't have her out here alone. I've never paid attention to the building across the street from her apartment. That's where these people came from.

Daphne laughs a little, but her cheeks are red. "Can you wait at the alley door? I need a minute. Unless you have something to tell me."

The first guard confers with the other one over her head. "We'll meet at the door," he tells her. Both of them jog across the street. One of them stays at the curb. If they both went to the alley door, they'd lose sight of her. Daphne doesn't come close to the car again. She's out of reach.

"I have to go." Her dark eyes mirror the dis-appointment in her voice. She would have gone with me. She would have done it, if she had another minute. I don't let this frustration show on my face. I won't show it to her at all. It's my patience that will be critical now. Daphne can't get the idea that a minor disruption like this one will make me lose interest.

"Go, then, little painter."

Her lips part. She takes a small, shivering breath. It's too cold for her to be out here. She should be with me. The flush in her cheeks gets another shade darker. Fuck me, it's perfect. Daphne hooks a hand in the neck of her hoodie and pulls. She could still get in. Could still run into my arms...

"Okay," she says. The word makes almost no sound.

She makes a quick turn and checks for traffic, then darts across the street. As soon as she's at the first security guard, he speaks to her. "Why?" I see her ask. I don't see his answer.

"Enough," I tell Logan.

"You sure?"

It won't be enough, nothing will be enough, until I have her. I'm sure I want her next to me instead of walking up the stairs to her apartment. I'm sure I need her in my sight. That's all I'm fucking sure of.

"Yes. Let's go home."

Chapter Twelve

Daphne

Gerard is waiting for me at Leo's front door. It snowed on the way here, flakes swirling against the windshield. I don't know how I'm supposed to feel. Being irritated feels wrong, but then so does being happy. I didn't have plans to come over today. I had a day off from the gallery.

And there was Emerson.

I was awake when his car showed up across the street. A dark-colored SUV that could not have been more conspicuous across from the gallery. At first I thought it might be one of Leo's, but when it got brighter I could see that it wasn't black, it was a really dark shade of gray.

Come with me.

The thing is, I wanted to go. I wanted to step out of my life for a minute and into his. Find out what he spends all his time looking at with those blue-green eyes.

I want to watch you paint it.

From a bedroom, I bet.

Emerson's expression changed when I asked him if that was all he wanted. I was already shivering, or it would have sent a new shiver down my spine. His eyes darkened, a certain fire catching there. Whatever else he wanted to do, it was dirty. Reckless, probably. I've never done that kind of thing. I've never gotten into the car of a practical stranger and let him take me to his house. I've never done the kinds of things I saw in his eyes.

If Leo sent security to bring me here over Emerson, I don't know what I'm going to do. Yell at him, maybe. Be furious. All I did was stand in the street and talk. But no, no—I'm not going to go in angry. That won't help anything. Though it does piss me off, not knowing what's happening. I'm once again in the dark. I won't be mad. I'm irritated. That's what.

I take the steps at a jog. "Hi, Gerard."

"Daphne."

He opens the door for me and we both step inside. Gerard holds my purse while I take off my coat. "Did something happen? Is that why I'm here?"

"No one went to the hospital."

I fake a glare at him. When Leo got home

from the hospital, Eva brought me with her to visit. I told Gerard I'd hold him personally responsible if Leo went to the hospital again and I was the last to know about it. Leo and Eva laughed at me for making threats. I guess they were right. I didn't make a good one. I was too specific.

"He's in the den," Gerard says. I take my purse back and drop it on a table near the coat closet.

To the den I go.

The second I step through the door, all my irritation dissolves. Leo stands at the window, the courtyard behind him. He looks like shit. Eva wasn't kidding about how bad things must have been. His eyes look too bright, like he might still have a fever. I saw him like this once. I hated it then, and I hate it now, and the only thing to do is go across the room and hug him. He's wearing a sweater. Good. He won't be trying to go to his office today. He shouldn't leave the house.

He bends down when I get close. Squeezes me tight. *You should have let me come over*, I want to say.

"Oh my god, Leo, you can't just summon me here. I'm fine. You could have texted me to ask if I was fine." Instead of the whole show outside my apartment. I thought the guards were going to confront me about Emerson. Insist on doing a background check or something. I let go of him, and he turns me around with his hands on my shoulders and takes me to the sofa.

Haley's there with a blanket over her and a book in her lap. She sits up as I come closer and tucks the blanket in tighter, like a shield. She also looks like shit. A sheen of tears is in her eyes. We've talked a couple of times, and I like her a lot. She's good. It's not good that she looks like this. That they both look like this.

"Hey, Daphne."

My stomach turns. I feel lightheaded, off-balance. Doomed, almost. This is what I get for wanting to know things. "Something happened."

"Caroline sent one of her people here," Leo says. He's leaned forward in his chair, his hands clasped in front of him. My mouth falls open as the words sink in. Caroline Constantine already sent someone here to shoot him. That wasn't enough? Images of a gun battle fly through my mind, but that can't have happened—everything looked normal when I came through the front doors.

"Did they come inside?"

"No. They didn't have to. Caroline's people

put together a plan to cause a diversion and distract my security while Haley went out to meet her brother." Leo's teeth snap together. His jaw works. He's trying to be calm. "They took her when she stepped outside the gates."

The blood drains out of my face, and I can't look at him anymore. I look at Haley instead. She's watching me, toying with the cover of her book with her thumbnail. "Took you where?"

"Caroline's house," she says.

My brain refuses to work. I thread my fingers together in my lap. "I don't understand. Caroline's your family. She sent someone to kidnap you?"

It makes more sense that she sent someone to kill my favorite brother. Their family hates ours. This thing Leo has with Haley—it transcends that somehow.

"Yes."

They sent someone here. To take her. And it would have had to be forcible, because she wouldn't leave on her own. She stayed with Leo when he was shot. Eva told me she was absolutely covered in blood in the hospital waiting room. She hardly slept while he was there, or when he was sick. Whatever crazy shit is happening, she loves him. The specifics of what this means slam into me. *They took her* means someone, probably a man, put his hands on her against her will and brought her to Caroline.

"Did they hurt you?" Maybe I shouldn't ask, but I want to know. I need to know what happened. I'm in the room now.

"No," Haley says.

"Don't lie." Leo sounds like something hurts, which is to say that he sounds angry, but I know he's not. He looks at Haley like he can't bear what happened to her. It was more than what she said. My heart pounds.

"I'm not lying." Her voice is soft.

"Don't. Lie." His is hard. Insistent. Why now? Why does he want me to know what happened now? He keeps things from me all the time.

I don't dare breathe while they look at each other. The space between them seems like too much. Like they're sitting apart because all they want to do is collapse into each other.

Haley takes a deep breath and looks back at me. "It's complicated," she says. "Nobody hit me. But it was still—" For a split second, her eyes go wide, as if she can't stand to remember. It wasn't that long ago the two of us were sitting in this den, talking. This was the look on her face when she thought I wanted her to tell me about the day Leo was shot. Now, she shakes her head and tries to smile. She can't.

"I'm sorry." Tears come to my eyes. Honestly, why? Why are people so terrible? "I'm sorry, Haley. I don't—I'm sorry."

I don't know what to say. Every woman grows up knowing that her life could be in danger at any time. All of us. We all know that, even if we have protective older brothers who do their best to keep us out of harm's way. It's still a shock when it happens.

"It's okay," she whispers.

"It's not," Leo says. "That's why you're here." I meet my brother's eyes and find fury there. "It's not safe for you. For any of us."

"I'm perfectly safe," I hear myself argue. My face heats. Is this how he brings up Emerson, then? "Nobody's messing with me. Nobody even really knows I'm a Morelli, because I'm not—" *Not like you.* That's what I'm going to say. I don't, though it's true. People know Leo. Nobody knows me. "I'm not open about it. Nobody's even been in my apartment, except—"

Shit.

Leo's eyes narrow. He sits up and folds his arms over his chest.

And waits.

There's no waiting him out. He's the king of frosty silences, which is why I think it's absolutely ridiculous that our father never caught on to what he was doing all those years. If Leo smashed a vase or put a book through a window, it was because he meant to cause a scene. He wanted Dad to look in his direction, and it always worked. I'm never going to out-silence him. It's not a contest I want to win.

I let out a sigh. "Except for one person."

"Except for one man." My cheeks burn. Leo nods. He saw. No hiding it now.

"Nothing happened," I insist, and let go of Haley's hand.

"Bullshit. Explain."

I bite my lip. Pull my hair back over my shoulder. I glance over at Haley, but she doesn't seem judgmental. She's got her thumbnail on the cover of her book again. There's no good way to do this, so I'll get as close to the incident as I can. No need to mention the gallery or how he parked outside this morning.

"I wasn't even there. He just left something for me. A gift."

A gift that was previously worth millions of dollars. Destroyed with black spray paint. All because I said I didn't like the painting. In reality, I hated that painting. I've always hated it. Lehmann was a piece of shit, and nobody should care that he was good at painting the ocean. Emerson's the only person who's ever done anything about it.

My face has to be so red. So is Leo's. He's pale from being shot and being sick, so it's obvious as soon as it starts. I knew it would be bad. This is worse. He's so upset that he's working overtime to hide it. That's what people don't understand. It's always the worst when it's quiet. A scene from Leo always serves another purpose, but if he tries to keep himself in check, then he really is angry.

"You have a fucking stalker." His voice is even. Light. We could be at dinner at our parents'. It scares me to death.

"No! No." I can't stop myself from grabbing at my collar. I need something to hang on to. "He just—he likes my paintings. He buys a lot of them. You know. Like a collector."

"He wants to collect your body in his basement, Daphne. He doesn't want your paintings. Men don't want your art. They're all sick fucks who want to use you for their own purposes. They'll discard you when they're finished, if they haven't murdered you first."

I lift my chin. Men might be terrible as a whole, but Emerson isn't. He's not. An old defensive anger presses at my lungs. "Oh? Like you're going to do to Haley?"

"No," Leo snaps. I flinch at how harsh it is, how mean it sounds, and it doesn't help that I feel like an asshole. For suggesting it to him. For still being pissed off. "Not like me with Haley."

Haley lets out a breath. This can't be comfortable to watch. I'm not comfortable, and neither is Leo, and she's sitting in the middle of what feels like a very old fight. Leo thinks I'm not old enough to be a good judge of men. Maybe I'm not, but I haven't had much of a chance. I could have taken chances, like Sophia, but it would worry him and I don't want him to worry, I want—I don't know what I want.

"He's not dangerous," I tell Leo.

"That's. Fucking. It." He stands up and goes to the door of the den. Throws it open. Gerard's waiting there. Guarding the door, it looks like. "Send a team to Daphne's apartment. Clear it out."

Oh my god. He's not serious. I came here for one conversation. I didn't come here for everything to be turned upside down. Leo turns around and finds me staring at him. Raises his eyebrows.

He comes to stand in front of the couch, in the middle of the den.

"What did you tell him to do?" I'm asking because he can still stop all this, if he wants. He can.

"I'm sending a team to get your things. You're moving in with me."

"Leo, no!" I scramble off the couch and face him. I'm not doing this sitting down. What the hell? He's so out of line right now. "I'm fine in my apartment. You have security there, too."

"I'm firing all of them. It will take some time to find replacements."

"Why? Why? I like them." I don't know them that well, but they've been fine. They mostly leave me alone. We get along that way.

"Because they let a stalker into your apartment to leave a gift. What's next? Are they going to let him in to watch you sleep? Shower?" It doesn't feel good to be mad at him when he's so wrung out. Everything is right on the surface for him. They've lived through a nightmare, my brother and Haley. But anger bubbles up anyway. He didn't tell me. He didn't tell me anything, but now he's going to dismantle my life in the name of safety.

"How is it better if you're the one watching

me sleep?"

"I'm not going to watch you sleep. I don't care if you sleep. Stay up all night, if you want."

"I want to stay in my apartment. I belong in my apartment. I'm fine in my apartment." The worst part is, I know he's right. I know it's not good that Emerson came inside, and the team didn't notice. They didn't stop him. They failed at doing their jobs.

"Will you be fine when you wake up to him standing over your bed one night?"

"Leo—" Maybe I would. He's not like Leo says. I can't explain that to him. There's no explaining it. Not now.

"Will you be fine if you wake up gagged and bound? Tell me." Ice fills the pit of my gut. How did Haley wake up at Caroline's house? Was it that bad? Was it worse?

"That's not going to happen." I'm telling Leo. I'm telling myself. Those things are not going to happen.

He steps in closer so I have to look up at him. I hate this. I hate that we're not on the same side. "And will you be fine if I have to come identify your body after he's murdered you? I'm the one who would get that call, by the way. Would that be all right, Daphne?"

I want to say something snippy and cutting. For all of a second. But from this close, I can see it now. Fear. In my brother's eyes. He's not afraid of anything, but if he was, this would be it. He's being such an asshole because of this thing he's named. Receiving the call that something had happened to me that he wasn't there to stop.

Tears sting my eyes. I blink them back. "He's not going to kill me." I drop my collar, but my hands turn into fists at my sides. "He's not like that."

"Tell me his name, and I'll tell you if he's like that."

It hurts too much to look at him. "I'm not telling you his name."

"Do you even know what it is?"

"Yes. I'm just not telling you. You'd go after him."

"He probably deserves it."

Silence falls. I steal a glance at Leo. He looks at Haley and something in his face softens. I can't fight with him right now. It's not the time. And some tiny part of me is relieved that he's alive to be so overbearing.

"You are ridiculous," I tell him.

"Good," he says.

I run my hands over my hair and try to put

aside my resentment. Make things light again. "How long am I supposed to stay here?"

"Until he forgets about you." Leo's so gentle when he says this that I know he means it. He really does want Emerson to forget all about me.

"Like you're going to forget about Haley when she's gone?" I tease.

Leo frowns. "It's different."

I roll my eyes. "It's different because you love her."

This was maybe too far. Leo grits his teeth. "This isn't about me."

"Isn't it?" For the first time in this conversation, I feel like we're on even footing. I might even have the upper hand. This talk about loving Haley has struck a nerve.

Leo's expression shutters. Goes hot and dark. "This is about you being in over your head. I always knew you were I, but I never thought you were a fool." He's not like this. Not with me. A hurt gasp flies out of me, but I can't think of a thing to say back. There's nothing I want to say back. "You want to end up on a true crime podcast? Not on my watch. I'm sorry if I ever gave you the impression you had a choice in the matter. You're staying here. End of story."

"Honestly?" My throat is tight with tears.

"Honestly?" Honestly nothing. I have nothing to say. I push past him and go out. I'm not far down the hall when Leo catches up with me. "Stay away."

"Daphne."

I stomp out into the foyer and wrench my purse from the table. I'm not going to leave. I'm not even going to try it. I round on him instead. "Are you even going to apologize?"

Leo has his hands in his pockets. "I'm sorry."

I stab a finger at him. "You're being a dick. And I'm not foolish."

"You're not," he agrees. "I shouldn't have said that."

What he doesn't say is *I'm tired. I'm afraid. Everything is falling apart.* He wouldn't say those things, though. Not to me. Maybe not to anyone.

"You're taking me out of my entire life."

"The tower suite is ready for you." Leo takes his hands out of his pockets and runs them over his face. An old memory snags in my mind, but I can't catch it. "The one with the sitting room."

I like that room. I found it after he moved in and said it should be a guest room. It's in one of the towers. It goes up above the rest of the house, hence the sitting room.

"The sitting room is a studio now," Leo mentions. "Tons of windows. Paint. Canvas."

"I thought you only just decided I was staying."

He shrugs. "I had it done a while ago. In case you ever wanted to stay."

I draw myself up to my full height. I still feel small. "Thank you."

"You're welcome." Ugh. This is the worst. This stilted conversation. Morelli politeness in Leo's house.

"I'm still angry."

"You're still alive," he points out, and then he turns and goes back to Haley.

CHAPTER THIRTEEN

Emerson

MICHAEL IS THRILLED about my next gift for Daphne. This one costs five million, and he is beside himself with joy that I'm not going to spray-paint the fuck out of it. We go through our ritual. I confirm that it's a Giorgia Russo original. Money goes from my account to his. I allow his assistant to take the piece, heavily wrapped and protected, to the SUV.

Streetlights are coming on in the dying afternoon on the way to Motif.

It's a violent painting. A woman slashes against demons, knife held high in the moments before a killing blow. The antithesis of Lehmann. It represents the artist's strength, instead of her fear. It represents Daphne's strength.

Neon signs shine through the tinted windows, little bars of color across my lap. Across my gloves. It reminds me of stained glass. Of light moving behind a closed door. One side illuminated, then the other.

I'll give it to her myself.

I didn't get to see her face when she discovered the ruined Lehmann. This is more important. Especially in light of how we were interrupted. I'm not going to be scared off by a couple of men in suits.

Logan parks directly in front of the gallery. I go to the back of the SUV and take out the painting myself. It's smaller than the Lehmann piece, but it feels heavier in my hands. It means so much more. Warmth from the front windows of Motif spills across the wrapping. Her hands will be on this soon. Pink in her cheeks. Light in her eyes.

A thin layer of snow cushions the sidewalk. The front door to Motif lets out a gust of heat into my face. They've turned it up. Daphne shivered in the cold next to my car window. She won't be doing that here, no matter what she's wearing. Robert looks up from his ledger and adjusts his beret.

"Mr. Leblanc. The showing with Nora—it was incredible." He puts both his hands to his chest. "I can't thank you enough."

"Where is she?"

He chews at his lip. Waits until I'm at the counter. "She's not here."

"Don't lie to me."

Robert closes the ledger. "I'm not lying. She was supposed to open this morning. I got here at one and the door was still locked."

Nervousness crawls at the pit of my gut. She knew the security guards who came out to the street. Daphne wasn't afraid of them. One of them said something about it being time to go. I didn't get the impression it was permanent, though. Security moves people around from time to time. Not in a way that makes them miss their shifts at a job they love. Daphne loves her job here. She loves painting. The commission thrilled her.

"Is she sick?"

Robert shakes his head. "I haven't heard." His brow furrows, like he's deciding whether or not to say. "I don't know, Mr. Leblanc."

Well, what the fuck? The painting feels oversized in my hands now. I feel foolish for bringing it here. I was so worried that she'd think I'd given up. I assumed she'd still be here. Even with the security thing happening. I thought she would be where I left her.

"If there's anything I can do—"

"No."

I need more information, and I'm not going

to get it from Robert. The most I can get from him is a promise to call me when she comes back. I go out the door to Motif. Cross the sidewalk. Wrench open the back door of the SUV. Logan startles. "Mr. Leblanc—"

"Stay where you are." I shove the painting into the back seat and get in after it. My heart tries to race, but I don't let it. I breathe deep. "Drive three blocks and pull over."

Logan doesn't ask any questions. He drives three blocks and stops in front of an alley. I take it to the next block. Aging brick. Wet concrete. Tracks in the snow. Snowflakes like moths around street lamps. The bottoms of the clouds burn orange from the pollution. They're like a hand over the city, those clouds. A big palm keeping everything in. It's not a small enough space. There are too many factors to control beneath the dome of the sky. A courier on a bike is a collection of angles, his bag a protrusion on one side. Chain wasn't meant for riding in winter. Every rusty squeak bounces back from store windows. Two blocks. One block.

The alley by Motif is empty. I keep my pace the same on the way to her door. No signs of security guards at the building across the street.

Count to three. Pick the lock. This door lets

me out onto a landing between the two doors. Robert must have been about to close when I came in, because he's not there now. No lights on in the back room. No ambient glow from the front of the gallery. The staircase up to Daphne's floor creaks in the middle, but not at the sides. I take them two at a time.

Her navy-blue doormat greets me in front of her door. Last time I was here, she had some canvases stacked at the end of the hall. They're not here now. She could have taken them inside her apartment to paint. It wouldn't be out of the ordinary for an artist to get lost in a piece.

Forget her shift at the gallery. If there's one thing Daphne loves more than working at the gallery, it's making art. I know that about her. It's in every picture that was taken of her at college and in everything she paints. It's possible to get evocative works out of hate, or even spite, but it's rare. Daphne doesn't strike me as a spiteful person. A person with secrets, yes. A person too innocent for the world, yes. But spite? No. That's not where her art comes from.

I stand on the doormat and hold my breath. My heart picks up in opposition, but it settles.

No light comes from around the doorframe, suggesting that there are no lights on inside. I wait a few minutes for my eyes to settle. It could be she's painting in low light, at her window easel, but I don't think so. The building's heat turns on again with a metallic rumble.

The only sound.

No footsteps. No music. No light.

I count to ten and pick the lock.

I was certain she wasn't here when I left the Lehmann piece. I'm not certain now. The best-case scenario is that she's painting and has lost track of time. The worst-case scenario is that she's sick, or hurt, and somehow no one from that security firm has noticed.

It doesn't take long to get the door open. The knob is smooth under my hand. It turns without resistance.

It's not right, and I know it from the first step. The sound is different. So different that I reach for the light switch on the wall. The light burns my eyes and I blink it away.

She's not here. And neither are her things. Her sofa is still here. Nothing else. I make a right into her kitchen and pull open the cupboards one by one. No teacup in the sink. No dishes in the cupboards. The dish towel from above the sink is gone. Her refrigerator hums in one corner. Empty, except for three bottled waters in a lower shelf that was clearly overlooked.

A loud buzz in my ears. It slowly resolves into a rush of blood. My footsteps echo on the way through her bedroom. The mirrored door of the medicine cabinet hangs open. Empty, empty, empty. A bare mattress is all that's left in her bedroom. No comforter tugged up to the pillows. No clothes in the narrow closet.

The scent of her is almost gone. So weak it's like she wasn't here at all. They've left her lace curtains. Whoever came through here didn't bother to take the curtains. I find myself at the window without any impression of the steps it takes to get there. Lace crumples in my hands. It's rougher than it looks. I half-hope to see her on the sidewalk below me, coming home, but what would she come home to? There's nothing here. I'm the only thing waiting.

Anger scorches the inside of my ribs. It's all claws and teeth. Three-dimensional and violent. A sound—the lace curtains beginning to tear. I let go of them, but what's the fucking point? She left this place. She left me. To a place I can't find her.

What was I thinking? *Go, then, little painter.* I told her to go. I should have known better than that. The first rule of acquisition is to keep the object in your sights. She makes me unreasonable.

She makes me forget the rules of my life. My anger shouts all this down. It's like heavy footsteps on another floor of the house. Always threatening, never coming close. Not until they do and by then it's too late.

What if it's too late?

What does it matter if she knew those security guards? What if I was wrong, and they weren't hired by her family at all? People have been known to play fucked-up games for months on end. Years. Long enough to convince an innocent like Daphne Morelli to trust them. Or—another awful possibility. She was safe with them, but isn't anymore. I've read her file. One time. Fifty times. The family has wealth, which means they have enemies. Robert doesn't know where she is, or else he's too afraid to talk about it. I don't know what it means. I don't know what the fuck it means.

I search her apartment again. Every shelf on every cupboard. The cheap plywood shelf in her closet, which I'm almost certain Daphne can't reach without a stepstool. Beneath the sink in her bathroom. I want an explanation. Where did you go, little painter?

Where?

There's nothing. Of course there's nothing. She wouldn't leave a note. Not here. I turn all the lights back off and pace. There is no light in the hall to show the shape of her door. It's black around the edges, which should mean safety. It should mean everything is all right. All it means now is that she's not out there.

She didn't plan to leave. My legs are heavy, dragging me down, but I don't dare sit on the couch. It feels like disturbing a crime scene, which is ridiculous. If this is a crime scene, it's ruined. I've touched everything. I choke down a laugh.

Force myself to stand still.

Okay. Daphne didn't plan on leaving. If she had a plan, she would have told Robert. She would not have left him to discover that she hadn't arrived for her shift. She'd have called, or texted. Maybe he knows more than he's letting on. It's not much more, though. A man who suspected murder, or who had carried it out himself, would have a haunted look to his eyes. Robert was worried about money. Mine, specifically.

That's not a guarantee she's all right.

I can't think.

Not until I go back into her bedroom. Put my back to the wall next to that absurd open archway and sit down on the floor. There's not much room between the wall and her bed. Enough for the bathroom door. I have to let this anger burn itself out. I can't think like this when it's out of control. It's an animal thing, that feeling. It makes the world press in. Every object transformed into razor-sharp edges. Not enough room to escape. So what if it feels like breathing in hot coals? So what if I can't focus on a single detail? My eyes have adjusted to the dark, but there's nothing here to see. A bedframe. An empty mattress.

Daphne might not have come back. If she left with people she trusts, then she might have her phone with her.

The number was not included in the dossier. Cell numbers can be difficult. They're easily changed, and I would bet that Daphne doesn't have her own phone plan.

I lock the door behind me when I leave. Go down the stairs to the landing between two doors. It's a cheap gallery. A cheap place. They have a set of keys for the alley door, a set of keys for the front. Any shoddy security system is likely to be focused on the front doors, not back here. Every sound is magnified now. The floor creaking under my feet. Wind against the alley door. Soft clicks from the lock pick on the knob. Focusing on this makes the emotions more bearable. More like a still life. Less like a fucking storm.

Once I've opened the door, once I've stepped inside into the quiet, I take out my phone and turn the brightness on the screen all the way down. The flashlight will be too conspicuous. It's a few steps from the back room to the counter. The beaded strands at the door are a minor irritation, and I'm there. Robert's ledger is in its place, the cover closed. Motif uses a simple register and an app for credit card purchases. What I'm looking for is in the first drawer on the right. A sticky note with the edges curled.

Daphne, it reads. Along with her number.

Below that—

Security. I take that number too. I won't call them and ask where she is. That would force my hand. I file it away for later. Go back through those damned beads. Out through the alley. Three long blocks back to where Logan is parked. My nerves feel frayed. Coming apart. I hate that she wasn't there. I hate that I don't know. I hate that I have to wait to text her. I can't start now, when I'm leaping out of my skin.

Logan waits on the sidewalk in the cold, hands shoved in his pockets, a frown on his face.

"Mr. Leblanc," he says when he sees me coming. "Are you all right?"

"Get back in the car," I snap. *Stop looking at me.*

"Where—"

"Home." I get in and pull the door shut behind me. She won't be there, either. Not yet. "Now."

CHAPTER FOURTEEN

Daphne

I AM UNREASONABLY pissed off at my brother.

The anger keeps coming back again and again and again. Just when I think it's gone—there it is. Maybe this is what I get for only painting the ocean. I'm constantly painting waves and it feels like I'm caught on the shore with endless breakers coming in.

I spend most of my time in the studio above my room, trying to work it out on the canvas. Leo has brought all the paints and brushes and canvases from my apartment, and on top of that, he's stocked the studio with everything I could ever want. It's honestly infuriating. Painting my feelings doesn't work. Surprise, surprise.

I don't want to be an ungrateful asshole. That's the worst thing about this. Leo is trying to be nice. He is trying to be nice in the way that he has always been nice, which is actual kindness layered in with him being ridiculous. He knows I like good paint. How could I not? He knows I try to pinch pennies at my apartment, so if I have to be here, I won't want for anything.

It's just that a lovely prison is still a prison. I can't live my life here, shut away from the world. Leo doesn't understand that. All he cares about is keeping the world away from me.

"You sound like a dick," I tell the piece in front of me, then fling some Prussian-blue paint at it.

No one answers. There's no one here to answer. I'm going after an innocent canvas, and not even wholeheartedly. It's me who sounds like a dick. Leo, my perfect, overbearing, irritating brother has been gracious about the fact that I don't want to eat meals with him. His housekeeper, Mrs. Page, brings me everything on a silver tray. Coffee in the morning. Tea in the afternoon. Occasional snacks.

There's absolutely nothing to be angry about, except that I am angry. My chest aches with the thought of disappointing Leo. Being pissed off constantly has to be a disappointment. The fact that I'm suffocating here has to be a disappointment. If he even knows I'm suffocating. If that even matters.

Which, of course, it does. Guilt crawls up my spine and latches on. Even in the privacy of my pissed-off feelings, I can admit that Leo's reaction is reasonable. Part of me knows that. Emerson was way out of line. He broke into my apartment. It is not okay to break into someone's apartment, even if they are leaving you something you didn't know you wanted.

Part of me knows that. And part of me is still fascinated by him. I am. I'm fascinated by the way he tasted, which was so clean and good and not like a stalker should taste. I'm fascinated by the way he touched me. By the way he scared me. Everything about him fascinates me. I wanted to go with him, damn it.

I put my brush to the canvas and fix the splotch of Prussian blue, blending it in with the rest of the wave.

I don't like to be angry. It feels bad, and more than that, it feels risky. My parents' house wasn't a place I could go around being angry. That would get the wrong kind of attention, and anyway, I don't want it.

My phone buzzes in my pocket. Leo, probably. Inviting me to eat with him, probably. He doesn't come up here to badger me about it. He texts, and I either give him a one-word answer or tell him I'm busy or say nothing at all.

It's the middle of the night. He'll be up. I

could pretend I'm sleeping, though I'm in the studio in my nightgown. I couldn't make my eyes stay shut. It wouldn't surprise me if the message was a casual invitation for tea or something in his den. He doesn't seem to sleep that much. Plus, he's trying to patch things up with me. I haven't been letting it happen.

None of this feels right. I don't like using the silent treatment, especially with my brother. But saying nothing seems like a better option than saying what I want to say.

Even if I did say it, none of it would make any sense. *Stop keeping me here. I understand why you feel like you should do this. I know I'm not safe at the apartment now that someone broke in. I almost got in a car with him. Be mad at me, the way I'm mad at you. I don't want to be mad at you. Don't be disappointed. I don't want to care if you're disappointed.* All very rational and good, right?

I put down the brush and take out the phone.

It's not a text from Leo. I don't have this number stored in my phone.

That doesn't matter. He's announced himself in the first text, the way he stood up tall in the gallery and looked me in the eye when I stepped into the room.

It's Emerson, the text reads.

My hands shake. He got my number some-how. Robert isn't supposed to give it out. I let the phone drop back onto the table that holds all my paints.

Emerson: Daphne.

Where is he right now? Sitting in his SUV outside my apartment? At his house by the beach? I can see him with his head bowed over his phone. His wetsuit from when he was surfing. Maybe he's standing at the shore now despite the whipping wind. Maybe he has his phone in one hand and his surfboard in the other, his feet crunching on snow-covered sand.

Emerson: Are you okay?

My heart clenches. I expected anger from him, not concern. More anger wells up alongside the ache in my chest. It's not only Leo I'm pissed at. It's me, for telling him anything in the first place, and it's Emerson. If he'd never fixated on me and broken into my apartment, I'd still have my apartment. I'd be going to my job at the gallery and selling paintings. I'd have my freedom.

Emerson: I'm calling the police.

I move so fast to pick up the phone that it

clatters to the floor.

> **Daphne: No**
>
> **Daphne: Emerson**
>
> **Daphne: Don't do that. I'm fine.**
>
> **Emerson: I don't believe you.**
>
> **Daphne: I swear. I'm staying with my brother!**
>
> **Emerson: Why?**

Because he thinks you're a psycho. I type it out and delete it. I wonder how he'd take that.

> **Daphne: Because I need some space from overbearing rich assholes**

Also, stop texting me in the middle of the night. Doesn't anyone have any sense of boundaries? *Or…keep texting me. More and more until I fall asleep with my phone.*

I toss my phone onto the table, another wave breaking over me. You know what? I'm done with this. I'm done with the silent treatment and avoiding the real problem, which is men telling me what to do.

Leo wants to talk about all this. Fine. We can talk.

I stomp down the stairs into the bedroom, sweep past my desk, and go out into Leo's giant hallway. It glows with moonlight coming in from his courtyard and low lights. The plush carpeting makes it impossible to stomp, so I give that up. I can act out my righteous anger with soft footsteps. My guest suite is at the opposite corner of the house from his bedroom. I don't see anyone on the way there, which isn't surprising. It's late. Too late to be doing this. I storm past a moment of hesitation. It would be better in the morning. It would be smartest to sleep on it and go down and talk to him at breakfast. But I don't feel good, and I don't feel smart. I'm at my wits' end being this pissed off.

Leo's bedroom door appears quicker than I thought it would. I take a deep breath and let it out. Anger got me here, but it will get me nowhere with my brother.

His door opens softly. It's not locked. Light angles in from behind me. "Leo?"

The sound reaches me at the same time the light reaches his bed. Something like a gasp.

Someone else is in his bed.

It's not Leo.

Leo doesn't have scars like that. There are so many I can't tell one from the next. Even in this half-light they're red and glaring, almost like burns. I catch a glimpse of Haley's hair. Someone must have gotten in. Someone is attacking her, right in front of me.

I try to scream, but the sound comes out terrified and garbled. What was I going to say? I don't know, I don't know. She doesn't need a warning. She needs Leo to be here, to fight off whoever this is—

The man picks up his head from where it had been, at the side of her neck, I think.

"What the hell, Daphne? You throw a tantrum for days and now you want to talk in the middle of the night? Get out."

It's him. I can see his face now, his eyes. Frustration burns there, hot and unfiltered. I can't move. Leo blinks. The anger's gone, but it's been replaced by something else—the same shock and horror I feel right now.

"Jesus. Daphne—"

I don't wait to hear what he says. I force myself to go. To run. All the way to the opposite side of the house, my gut churning and my skin gone cold. It looked so bad. It looked so, so bad. Something terrible happened to him. His skin. It must have been so awful. I throw myself through the door of my bedroom and stumble to the desk. Drop into the seat.

The tears come fast, one after another. I fold

my arms on the smooth wood and rest my head and cry.

Jesus Christ.

It's so bad.

I don't know how much later it is when the door glides across the carpet. "Daphne."

Leo.

I pick up my head from my arms and watch him come into the center of the room. He's dressed now. Soft black pants. A soft black shirt. My chest hurts.

"Who did that to you?" The question feels like a sore throat. "Was it Dad?"

Because if it was, because if our father did that…

Leo folds his arms over his chest, and it strikes me how tired he looks. It's late, but there's more to it than that. Shadows under his eyes. Something near my spine goes numb and buzzing.

"There are some things it's easier not to know," he says, his voice tight.

"Who was it?" I might as well be breathing through a straw. "And what—what—"

My brother takes a deep breath. He looks past me, into the corner of the room. Pain is a ghost light in his eyes. He uncrosses his arms and puts his hands in his pockets. "It was Caroline

Constantine. With a whip."

It sinks in slowly. So, so slowly. Horror like a boulder. Confusion like a heavy chain. She did that to him. All those wounds. One by one. The time it must have taken. "Why?"

"A long time ago, I got involved with her."

"Involved?"

The look he gives me says what *involved* means.

"That's not possible. You would never. You hate the Constantines."

"She was convincing." My skin goes cold. Leo continues. "It wasn't how I thought it would be. She got upset when I tried to end it. Crazy. She begged to see me one last time, and I fell for it. She had whiskey waiting when I got there. Drugged. It was how she got what she wanted. Sex, and then..." Leo gestures over his shoulder. "After she was done, she sent me home again."

No.

"She drugged you because she—because you—" I shake my head. You don't drug someone who wants to be there. You don't whip someone for trying to leave. But some people do. The world is full of people like that. Every woman alive knows the danger. It couldn't have happened to Leo. "She made you do it?"

A shadow moves across his eyes. "I agreed. In the beginning." Hearing this is like swallowing glass. It has to feel the same way to say it. "Not so at the end."

"But…" I'm beginning to understand something, and I don't want to. *A long time ago, I got involved with her.* "When did this happen?"

"Daphne…"

"When?"

"When I was fourteen."

I stand up without knowing why. Leo crosses the room and picks up something from the floor. A wastebasket that sits at the side of my desk.

"That's too young," I manage, and then bile surges up along with my dinner.

He holds my hair back from my face. And that's maybe the worst thing. That he's standing here saying things like *it's okay, Daph* and *don't worry* and *I know* when it's him who has to live with it, and I didn't know, I didn't know. When it's over I burst into tears.

Most of my memories from that time are hazy and indistinct, but there are a few that stand out in perfect clarity. Me, standing at the side of Leo's bed, shaking him and shaking him. I'd had a bad dream. I'd dreamed I was still in trouble from earlier in the week. But he wouldn't wake up. He looked too pale, too deeply asleep, and that scared me more than the dream did.

Leo goes to the door and murmurs something to someone waiting outside, and then he takes me through to the connecting bathroom. He puts toothpaste on my toothbrush and gets an elastic for my hair and collects a glass for water.

I can't stop crying. I've had a lot of practice turning off tears, but this time I can't do it. He takes me back to the bedroom and waits while I sit at the side of the bed. Then he pulls up the chair from the desk.

He doesn't lean back in his chair, and I notice it now. All the times I've seen him. In his house. In our parents' house. He's never tossed himself onto a couch or sat back in a church pew.

"Does it still hurt?" I want him to tell me it doesn't. That it looks worse than it is.

"It's hurt every day since it happened, Daph. My nerves are all fucked up."

"Jesus." I wipe away more tears. I might not be able to stop but I don't have to sob. Hurt coils around my heart. "Is it bad?"

"Yes."

That *yes*, from him, might as well be a novel on how badly it hurts. He would never admit it if it wasn't terrible. "Am I the only one who didn't know?"

"No." He looks me in the eye. "I've told a very limited number of people. Eva and Haley. Gerard and Mrs. Page."

"But not me."

"Daphne." More hurt wells up at his tone. So damn gentle. "You were five."

"I'm not five now."

"I'm telling you now." His eyes flash, and my stomach crumples again. I am asking too much. "Jesus. I never wanted to tell anyone in the first place."

"Why did you tell Eva, then? Because she could handle it, right?" And I couldn't, no matter how old I got. He is my favorite brother. That doesn't mean he owes me his secrets. But he's been wrapped in pain for years and years, and I never noticed. How could I have missed so much?

He takes a breath and his gaze slips away again. Something's happening in his mind. To keep himself in control. I've seen him do this a hundred times. A thousand. I never knew what he was thinking about.

"Eva only knows because she was standing in the foyer when I got home. There was no hiding it. The blood had soaked through my jacket."

Another memory whispers by. The hallway at

my parents' house as a child. Frozen in place on the way to the bathroom. I'd heard a ghost. It sounded horrible to be a ghost. Like it hurt.

"There's no way she fixed that." Eva's only a little bit older than Leo, and definitely not a doctor. "You had to go somewhere."

"I didn't. We used rubbing alcohol."

Agony. It had to be agony. "And that was enough?"

"No. It got infected afterward. She had to drive me to the hospital while everyone else was out of the house."

"Oh my god. Was that—" Eva sitting next to me on the couch, her arm around me. *It's just a trip for school,* she said. *He'll be back soon.* "That was the trip for school."

Leo's mouth hints at a smile. "I'm surprised you remember that."

I'll never forget the trip for school.

I don't want to tell him why.

"I remember more than you think."

His expression sobers. "I'm sure you do."

"You should have told me." My tears feel like plain salt now, burning into my skin. "You should have let me choose."

My brother reaches for my hand and holds it. "There wasn't a lot of choice to go around."

"You should have let all of us choose." Because. "You fought with Dad. You got hurt. And now I find out—now I find out it's on top of this."

"That was the deal," Leo says. "The more he came after me, the less he came after you."

"You could have said—"

He very nearly laughs. "Could have said what? *By the way, Daphne, Caroline Constantine attacked me. Could Dad beat the shit out of you this time?*" Leo shakes his head. "No."

"Leo."

"I was trying to give you a chance."

"To do what?"

"To be anybody in the world. Anyone you wanted to be." His voice thins out. "I didn't want you to have to be me. Angry all the time. Hurt all the time. It's exhausting." He squeezes my hand, and it's like watching a house of cards tumble to the ground. I've always seen Leo as invincible. Practically all-powerful. I didn't think about the cost. And this—this is costing him. There's a tension around his eyes that I assumed was irritation, but it's not. I know now. It's pain. "I can't let it happen, Daphne. I can't let this collector take anything from you against your will."

I stand up, and so does he, and this time when I hug him, I hesitate. He's always moving my arms at the last second. Always with his guard up. I thought it was because he was ticklish, or something like that, but it's the scars. My heart breaks all over again.

"I wish you would have told me. It hurts that you didn't say anything."

"I know."

"I'm still kind of mad."

"I know that, too."

I'm not going to fight him on this anymore. I'll stay. Guilt coats the insides of my lungs. It's hard to breathe like this. It was probably harder for Leo, all these years. It's the smaller moments that make me want to sob right now. I can picture Eva's face when he stepped into the foyer. The moment the rubbing alcohol touched his skin. Blood on the hem of a shirt. I imagine the ocean washing these thoughts away so I can sleep tonight. How has he lived like this? How?

"Are you pissed at me?"

Leo huffs a laugh, but it sounds sad. "No, sister mine. I'm not."

Chapter Fifteen

Daphne

About three glasses of champagne into Haley's birthday party, things start to feel easier.

The knowing is harder than I expected. It felt like a stone at the pit of my gut. Leo spent the last few days planning Haley's party with Eva. She was in and out of his house, on her phone, in his office. Every time I came down from the studio they were conspiring about one thing or another.

"What do you think, Daphne?" Eva asked me from one of the chairs in Leo's office. I had paint under my nails and some of it had gotten in my hair. "Gold and white or pink and white?"

Easy. "Gold. And tons of balloons. She deserves a ridiculous amount of balloons."

"I told you she'd vote with me." Leo was on his phone. On hold with someone, probably.

"Betrayed again." Eva laughed. "Make a decision on the food."

"Why would I do that when you're here?"

I always knew they were close. It makes sense. They're close in age. But there's so much more to it than that. Leo's secrets are so painful. They're so heavy. Eva doesn't just know them, she witnessed them firsthand. She carries them around with her. I don't know how they sat there talking about balloons and dinner menus like this thing didn't happen.

Knowing changes everything. It makes me reconsider my memories. The things I used to think. The look on Leo's face when I told him about Emerson coming into my apartment breaks my heart, in retrospect.

It's not as heavy tonight. We've all given up on dinner and now it's nothing but dancing. Haley's brother, Cash, approaches her on the dance floor. Somehow, he is here at this party.

I go over to where Leo's at the gift table with a plate of cake in his hands. "You let him in here after what he did?"

Not the most tactful, but that's champagne. I wouldn't say I was drunk. Pleasantly buzzed, more like. Maybe drunk. It's a birthday party. But it's a legitimate question. Cash called Haley and asked her to come let him in at the gate. That's when Caroline's people took her. I don't know the specifics of what happened while she was there, but I know they touched her. I know it shook her. Scared her. What I can't understand is how Leo forgave her brother for it.

"Yes." Leo cuts off a layer of frosting and eats it. "He wouldn't come unless I hired him his own bodyguard."

That explains the random guard standing by in a corner of the room all night. "To protect him from you?"

"Obviously."

I stare at Cash too long, because Leo nudges me with his elbow. "Caroline sent her new bulldog to their house and broke his ribs while their father was asleep. They threatened to do the same to the old man if he didn't help with Haley."

The champagne is really good, and what Leo's told me is very bad. It makes my heart ache for Cash. "You wouldn't have done it. Broken ribs or not."

"His father isn't like ours." Casual. While he's eating birthday cake.

"What do you mean?" A server goes by, and I take another glass of champagne. "You'd have let them beat up Dad?"

Leo raises an eyebrow at me. "I meant that Phillip Constantine doesn't have a violent bone in his body, so the broken ribs had to have been a shock. It was convincing for Cash. There were no good choices."

"What are you, some kind of saint?"

He snorts. "Hardly."

"You just…forgave him and invited him to the party?"

Leo motions to Haley and Cash with his fork. They're dancing now. "Look at Haley and tell me if my forgiveness is the top priority in this scenario."

Cash's movements are stiff. It hasn't been that long since the beating. But he's still trying. He puts out his hand and spins Haley. I don't hear what he says, but she laughs. "That was an accident. I thought there was a bug."

"She's your top priority in this scenario." I've tipped over the edge into definitely drunk.

"She wanted her family on her birthday."

"It's mostly us, though."

"I couldn't reach her older sister. Her father was too much of a risk. Cash was a hard sell, but…" His eyes soften as he watches Haley. "I gave her everything I could."

Eva whirls in from behind me. "Come dance," she says. "We're going to dance again."

Leo leans down to be heard over the music.

"For the record, Daph, I'd pick you over Dad every fucking time."

Then he strides out to where Haley is waiting and cuts in on Cash, who is immediately swept up by Elaine. Lucian and Elaine are absolutely ridiculous dancers. It makes me laugh, and laugh again, because everyone is afraid of Lucian. Here, in Leo's ballroom, he's...

I don't know how to describe it. He's so focused on Elaine that nothing else matters. Neither of them seems self-conscious. Elaine keeps pulling Cash in to dance with them, and he keeps trying to dance back out, but it's not happening. Everyone is drunk and happy.

Eva takes both my hands in hers and spins us both around. Her face is pink from champagne, her hair is coming out of its twist, and she's laughing. I don't see her laugh like this very much. I've always thought she was smart and serious and regal. It turns out she's also a hero, in her own way.

It's warm in the ballroom. Loud. Balloons bounce against everyone's feet. We've thoroughly destroyed the dessert table. Mrs. Page went to bed hours ago. Gerard keeps coming in and out, and so do the last of the servers.

The evening goes fuzzy. Something falls away

as we dance. It's not like the dinner party Lucian insisted on having after I got here, with everyone cutting glances at each other and sitting up straight. Maybe this is what it would have been like if our parents were normal. I've always loved parties. I never knew they could be like this.

"Are you okay?" Eva asks over the music. "You look so far away."

"Thirsty." We go over to the table, where there is ice water. I hold the glass in my hand and sway to the music. Eva's doing the same thing. We both look out at the party together. Lucian and Elaine are attempting to swing dance. Cash is calling out instructions. And Leo is actually dancing with Haley. When he spins her close, she rests her head on his shoulder. I can see her smile from here. After a minute she leans up to whisper in his ear, and the way he angles himself to answer her is so intimate that I don't feel like I should watch.

Leo looks over at us. He usually doesn't drink, but he's had one or two tonight. "Dance," he says.

Eva abandons her ice water.

"I'll be right there. I'm going to check my messages."

"Boo," Eva says, but she's laughing again, and then she's dancing with everybody else.

I get my phone from the dinner table and flip it over. The screen is hazy. Or I'm drunk. A few blinks and I can focus again.

My heart jumps into my throat.

Emerson: Tell me if you're okay.

Daphne: I'm perfectly fine!!

The music gets louder, and I can't believe, I honestly can't believe, that this is happening at all. Constantines in Leo's house. The way he looks at her. Lucian, being a goofball for once in his entire life. Longing squeezes at my heart. I want to be as close with someone as Leo is with Haley. I want that. I want it so much.

My phone buzzes in my hand.

Emerson: I'll send the police to check.

Daphne: Do NOT do that. My brother would freak out.

Emerson: Which brother?

I blink at the phone. Read it again. Cold awareness fights to get through the champagne drunk, but it can't quite make it. He knows I have more than one brother. He knows.

Daphne: Did you look me up on Facebook?

Three little dots float on the screen. I peek

over my shoulder to make sure he's not watching through the window. That's silly. He couldn't get into Leo's courtyard. There's no way he's watching me right now.

Emerson: Of course not, little painter.

It doesn't make me feel any better.
He's typing again.

Emerson: I don't need social media. I have a complete dossier on you.

Noise beats at my ears, so loud I think something's gone wrong with the music. It's not the music. It's my heart.

Emerson: I know your birthday

Emerson: Your social security number

Emerson: The tax ID number of the dummy corporation your father made to funnel money through when you were four years old

No, I type out. I don't get a chance to send it.

Emerson: I know what you think about at night.

I move my thumb over the button to block his number. To stop him from saying any of these things to me. To stop him from scaring the shit out of me. I could walk across the room right now and put my phone in Leo's hand. I wouldn't have to say anything out loud. It would be over. This insane, intense obsession—it would be done.

Daphne: Do you?

"Come dance," Eva calls.

"I'll be right there."

No new dots appear on the screen. I hold my breath. He makes me wait so long I have to let it out again. I have to keep breathing. Keep feeling the hairs pulled tight at the back of my neck.

The next text to arrive has no words. It's a picture. I curl my hand over the screen to hide it, but there's nothing illicit. It's the ocean at night. My breath catches. The nose of a surfboard pokes into the bottom edge of the frame.

I painted this. I didn't have a reference photo. He could be out there right now, frozen to the bone, diving into black water.

Daphne: That's not what I think about

I'm lying. I think about him on his surfboard all the time.

Eva can't tolerate this another second longer and she drags me back out to the dance floor. I've lost my champagne. She hands me another one. No one cares that I have my phone in my hand. I take pictures of the party so someone will remember it later. Leo and Haley are like two stars in orbit around one another. The later it gets, the more she laughs. He laughs with her. But there's something else in his eyes. Sadness, I think.

Another text.

Another picture.

A painting, hung on the wall of a house. A man's shadow over it. It's the painting I made for him. It's Emerson's shadow. It strikes me as unbelievably dirty, his shadow over my art like that. He owns it. It's his now. That painting is his little prisoner.

Daphne: Not that either...

This time, only a few minutes pass.

A third picture.

If Lucian noticed all the texting right now, I could truthfully say that it is another picture of the ocean. But this time, the ocean is viewed through a window.

A bedroom window.

I know instantly that this is Emerson's bed. Neatly made up. It's practically an invitation to destroy it.

Daphne: I think of your eyes in the art gallery

Emerson: When I kissed you?

Daphne: When you were watching me

Emerson: You liked it

Daphne: No, I didn't

Eva drags me to the dessert table and forces me to eat more cake. Leo and Haley follow, and Cash, and then Elaine and Lucian and somehow it escalates into plans for a personalized bouquet to be sent to the bakery. It's a perfect cake.

"You made the right call." Eva grabs my hand and looks deeply into my eyes. "I want you to know that."

My spine freezes. I'm drunk. Does she mean Emerson? "About what?"

"The gold and white," she says. Oh my god. The party decorations. "It's better than what I was picturing."

She wants to dance, so we dance.

Emerson: Tell the truth, little painter. Pretend I'm one of your canvases. I want to know what you need.

Daphne: I can't tell you that

Emerson: You can tell me anything.

I can't tell him anything. That's dangerous. It's dangerous for anyone, but especially for me. You have to really be able to trust a person to tell them everything. Leo and Haley have stopped dancing. They stand still in the middle of everything, his hands on her face, his eyes on hers. I can't hear a word of what he's saying. He trusts her with everything.

Daphne: What do you think about at night?

No answer.

No dots on the phone.

My eyes burn with how late it is, and how drunk I am. Leo shoos Lucian and Elaine into a car, which they barely see because they're too busy making out with each other. He helps Eva into a second one and stands there with the door open, talking to her for several minutes too long.

"I'm going to bed." I pull Haley in for a hug. "Happy birthday."

"Thank you." She squeezes me tight. "I'm so happy you were here. I really mean it. I loved it."

It makes my heart hurt. It makes me laugh. "I'll come to all your parties. But right now I have to go to sleep. I think I'll die if I don't."

"Me too." Haley laughs and lets me go. Her

face is pink and her eyes are bright, and I'm happy for her. After everything, she deserves this. "Night, Daphne."

I'm almost up the stairs when Leo comes into the foyer and picks her up in his arms. He makes it look easy. Like it doesn't matter if he got shot, it doesn't matter if he was sick. He won't let it show. She drops her head onto his shoulder.

Am I jealous? Maybe.

In the tower suite I toss my phone on the pillow and go to wash my face. Pins out of my hair. Dress off. Party's over. Time for a tank top and lounge pants. Time to get under the covers and dream of a man I shouldn't want. I'm not interested in over-the-top obsession like that. I want what Leo and Haley have.

I'm two steps from the bed when my phone lights up.

I freeze in place, goose bumps rising on the back of my neck. It's a coincidence. He's not watching.

On tiptoe, I approach the side of the bed and lean over to see the message.

It's from Emerson.

All it says is:

You.

CHAPTER SIXTEEN

Daphne

EVERYTHING FALLS APART.

That's how it goes, doesn't it? For one shining evening, everything is warm and good and right. And then it crashes to the ground.

A few days after Haley's birthday party, I come downstairs and Leo tells me she's gone. Which is impossible. He loves her. He's in love with her. He won't give me any details, so I go to Gerard, who says Leo sent her away. Something to do with her father being sick. With the Constantines.

It never stops with them. It makes me sick. I always thought the feud between our families was like the cliques at school. An easy way to belong, never with any teeth. But then—people got bullied out of school, didn't they? Not everyone had an older brother waiting in the wings to scare the shit out of anyone who tried anything with them. Not everyone was safe. Leo wasn't safe. I just thought he was.

After Haley leaves, Leo becomes a ghost. A shadow of himself. He doesn't come upstairs for four days. Doesn't go to his bedroom. Every afternoon I come down and knock on the door to his office. He looks at me with hollow eyes and tells me to go back to my painting. He keeps saying he's okay, but I know he's not.

I know, because Mrs. Page hovers outside the door, conferring with one of the cooks from the kitchen in hushed tones. Timothy, I think his name is. Gerard paces the halls. He walks miles, his mouth in a thin line.

And I paint. I paint waves upon waves, and then I cover them in white and start again. I paint until my fingers cramp. I paint until I can't stay awake anymore. The weather gets colder. The air inside the house feels like icicles.

Emerson: Talk to me.

I don't answer him. I don't know what to say. It feels wrong to be texting him. I'm afraid that if I text him, I'll tell him how afraid I am. I'll ask him to take me away.

Emerson: I know you're there, little painter.

He doesn't know anything. I can't tell him

anything.

On the fifth morning, I wake up early with my stomach in knots. I can't do this anymore. I can't watch Leo sit at his desk with that horrible blank expression. I can't do it. I'll tell him about Emerson. I'll tell him anything to make the fire come back to his face. I'll tell him, the way I always used to tell him everything, and he will come back to life.

The house is silent on the way downstairs. Everything has a sheen of white to it. Winter light. It's almost crystalline. I watch it play over Leo's wallpaper and think of how it might look on ocean waves. A storm coming in, maybe. Storms can be ominous, but in winter they wipe things clean. Fresh, new snow.

Emerson: Anything.

I push open the door to Leo's office.

Emerson: If you won't talk, I'll talk to you

Emerson: It's cold as hell on the water today.

Emerson: The beach is empty.

It's warm inside, but it looks cold. Light pours in from his courtyard. I can see everything. The book abandoned on a table by the fire. The glass paperweight I gave him when I was twelve. I found it at an art gallery and thought he would like it, and he's kept it since then.

Leo, dead on his desk.

My heart stops. He's not moving. You can see it when a person breathes. There's no motion in the room. He has his head in his arms, and his shoulders don't rise. There's nothing.

"Leo." I rush across the room, my blood running as cold as the snow outside. My phone falls out of my hand. "Oh, shit. Oh my god. Oh my god." A bottle of pills is upended on his desk beside a bottle of—I pick it up and stare at the label like it can give me an answer. Whiskey. "No, Leo. No." He didn't do this. "Oh, shit, what do I do? What do I—Leo. Please?" He can't have done this, he can't, he can't. He wouldn't. Not while I'm in his house. He would never want me to find him like this. "Leo—"

I put my hand out to shake his shoulder.

He's instantly in motion, shoving my hand away, getting to his feet, yelling. It shocks me to the core. He doesn't yell. He doesn't ever yell at me. "Don't touch me. Don't *touch* me!"

It's the most anguished I've ever heard him. Like I hurt him. Like he doesn't want to be alive.

"I thought you were dead." Tears run down

my face, and I can't stop them. I've never been so terrified. "You weren't moving, Leo. Have you been in here all night? Did you drink all of that?" I point at the bottle on his desk.

"Get out," he snaps at me. No color in his face. "Get the fuck out."

"No. I can't leave you in here. I thought you were dead. Did you try to kill yourself?" I don't know what to do. "You're—you're scary like this."

And he is. He's never scared me so much. I didn't think he ever would. My heart is trying to peel itself out of my chest.

Leo's face clouds over with regret, and pain. He sits down in his chair and balances himself with a hand on the edge of his desk. "I didn't try to kill myself. I'm fine."

"You're lying." I clear my throat to keep from sobbing. "You're so pale. And you were so still. I know you're not fine. I can see you." I go to the side of his desk and swallow more fear. I wanted to be independent, and strong, and now look at me. "I think I should call Eva. She would know what to do."

"She has her own heartbreak to deal with. Her own life." Her own heartbreak? What heartbreak? The scariest part is how resigned he sounds. Like he's known this for a long time. He knows one of

Eva's secrets. Like she knows one of his. It's too much to think about.

"Why don't you go to her?" My heart is breaking for him. I don't understand how he can love Haley the way he does and stay away from her. I don't understand how he can do this to himself. "Why don't you go to Haley?"

Leo rubs both hands over his face. "Because I love her."

"That doesn't make any sense." My hands shake now. I thought he was dead. "If you love her, you should be with her."

"My love for her is more than that. It's strong enough to let her go." He sounds like he can barely breathe. "She has a family. Those are her people. I was always fooling myself that she could be mine."

"Leo…" The world feels like it's tilted in the wrong direction. I want to tell him. I want the relief of not keeping a secret. I used to tell him everything, and now I think it might push him over the edge. I think it might be worse for him to know. Much worse. For him, not for me. I'm already living here. He's on the brink of total collapse.

His eyes look huge in his face. Too huge. "I'm sorry, Daphne." He waves at the desk. Grimaces at the pills. "For this."

"Have you slept? Since she…since Haley. Not like this. In your bed."

Leo shakes his head.

"Will you take a nap?" I take a deep breath and summon all the confidence I have. "We're obviously having dinner together tonight. You can't do this anymore."

"I'll go upstairs. Have the kitchen make whatever you want."

"I'm sending Gerard up to get you," I say to his back. His clothes are wrinkled. He's a wreck. Leo is never a wreck. "It's rude to be late for dinner."

He turns back and tries to smile at me. It flickers and dies before it reaches his eyes. "I wouldn't miss it for the world."

On the floor of Leo's office, my phone lights up.

Emerson: You can fly away any time, little painter.

Emerson: I know a place you could land.

Daphne: I can't leave

Emerson: Because you don't want to, or because someone is stopping you?

Daphne: I can't.

WATCHING LEO PICK at his food does nothing to make me feel better about this situation. He swears he slept. I don't know if I believe him. He still looks pale and drawn and nothing like my brother. My hands tremble every time I pick up my fork. I guess I'm not over finding him in his office this morning.

"You're not eating anything, Leo."

"I've eaten."

He's such a liar. "Okay, but you know you have to eat more than that. You're going to starve to death. Plus, it's good salad."

"I hate salad."

I drop my fork and put my hands over my eyes. I double-checked the menu with him earlier. I made Gerard go in and show him so I'd know he was alive. "Why are we having salad, then?"

"Penance."

A shout echoes down from Leo's foyer. "What is that?"

"Go up to your room." He gets out of his seat. "Put on some music and don't come down until the album's over."

Not a chance in hell. "You'll have to carry me there yourself."

"Might be a little short on time."

It's Leo's security team doing the shouting. Fear is a bitter taste on my tongue. If someone came in—if that someone was Emerson—

Gerard tries to stop us. "Go back," he says. "Go up."

We're two steps into the foyer when the police burst in. It's all I can do not to scream. Panic swells over my skin. Oh my god. Emerson actually did it. I told him I couldn't leave, and he sent the police to come see if I was okay. He sent the police to Leo's house. This is going to end in a war, or worse. Gerard sticks out an arm to keep me from going to Leo's side.

The police captain waves a piece of paper in Leo's face.

He doesn't react. "You're supposed to show me the warrant before you invade my house," he says.

The captain steps in closer. No one stands that close to Leo. No one gets in his face like that. "Mr. Morelli, we have a warrant to search your property for evidence of the kidnapping and captivity of Haley Constantine. We had reason to believe there would be interference with the collection of evidence, necessitating a no-knock entrance."

I open my mouth to tell them that I haven't been kidnapped when the meaning hits.

Haley. Not me.

"Her toothbrush is upstairs in the master bath, if you'd like to start there," Leo answers.

"My god. You have the right to remain silent, you sick fuck. Everything you say can and will be used against you in a court of law. You have the right to an attorney. If you can't afford an attorney, one will be provided for you. Do you understand the rights I've just read to you?" He's sneering at Leo. He looks disgusted. I know people don't like him. I know people are afraid of him. But this contempt—I've never seen it happen like this before. This openly.

"You didn't read them," Leo comments. "Let's strive for accuracy."

"Do you understand your rights?"

"Yes, Captain, I do. Everyone's body cameras on? Let's make this simple. I kidnapped Haley Constantine."

"Leo, stop. Let me go." I push Gerard's arm away and go to stand next to him. He can't do this. "Stop. Don't say that. You can't say this."

"Haley Constantine was my captive." The noise level in the room drops, and so does my heart. They want to hear him say this. They're all listening to him lie. "I held her here, and I didn't let her leave."

"Leo." Gerard cuts in. "That's not what happened."

But Leo doesn't stop. "I forced her to sign a contract with me in exchange for releasing her father from a business deal. I coerced her. Exploited her."

I put a hand on his elbow and pull. Hard enough to get his attention. "Don't lie to them, Leo."

"I'm telling the truth. God as my witness. I held Haley Constantine hostage."

"You didn't." Why is he saying this? She loves him. She loved him. I saw them at her birthday. "You didn't hold her hostage. She wanted to be here. What are you talking about?"

"I held her hostage. She wasn't free to leave. Or would you prefer if I called her a prisoner?" Leo's voice fills the foyer.

"It's not true." Tears spill over and run down my cheeks. He's not in his right mind. He shouldn't be doing this. "Stop lying. Stop, stop, stop."

Leo looks down at me, and his eyes are dead. Nothing there. Nothing left. "Sorry, sister mine. I'm not the man you think I am. I'm as bad as your collector. Worse. Dry your tears. They're not worth crying for me."

I let go of him and wipe my tears. Fine. I won't cry. Fine—but he can't do this.

"Anything else you'd like to confess?" Police are everywhere in the foyer. The police captain grins like he's won the lottery.

Gerard is on the phone to Eva. Explaining. It still doesn't make any sense.

"Leave her alone, Gerard," Leo says, voice flat. And then he laughs out loud. It sounds like he's coming apart at the seams. It sounds like the end of everything.

"Is this funny to you?" the police captain snarls.

"I'm entertained. Of course I am. You and thirty of your buddies are in my house, rifling through my things because you're so convinced I kidnapped a woman. Fine. I agree. I kidnapped her. It doesn't matter that she came here by herself, does it? Or that she's home with her family as we speak."

They're starting to leave now. So many officers. Boxes in their hands. It's sick. When the last one is out, the police captain checks behind him. Then he turns back to Leo.

"Charges are pending investigation, Mr. Morelli." He looks all around the foyer. "I bet you'll miss this place when we put you away."

Leo smiles at him, and it's like watching a wolf. I move to stand in front of him. No one should be seeing him like this, least of all this police captain. "Stop trying to scare us. You've done your job."

The police captain looks me up and down. Head to toe. It's not like when Emerson looked at me. It's disgusting. Leo growls behind me. "Get the hell out of here."

As soon as the front door closes, I turn to face him. "Why did you say that?" I'm pissed again. I'm so royally pissed. I don't understand. "Why did you say that you kidnapped Haley when you didn't? They're going to use that against you."

"Because it's true. So close to the truth, it might as well be true. I forced her to be with me. Did you think your brother was kind and noble? No, sister mine. I made her trade her body to save her father."

I can't believe it.

I can't.

He's out of his mind with grief. He misses her and he's lying. It's so reckless. It's so unlike him. I can't speak. I leave him standing there in the foyer. I don't know what else to do.

"I don't believe you," I say at the top of the stairs.

He can't hear me. No one can.

THE NEXT TIME I see Leo is two and a half hours later, from the door of his office. No more winter sun. Only firelight. He's sitting on the rug in front of his fireplace, silent tears streaking down his cheeks, Haley in his arms. She keeps wiping them away. Murmuring soft things to him. He can't take his eyes off her.

The office is a mess. The furniture is turned over, his desk in ruins, the glass paperweight shattered on the floor. A knife lies on the edge of the rug, near the paperweight. My heart might never stop racing.

I hear Eva come in through the foyer. She puts a hand on my shoulder and tries to control her breathing. "I couldn't get here in time." Regret colors her voice. "Are you okay?"

"I didn't see anything." I'm numb with relief, and with confusion. "He made me stay upstairs."

"That's good," she whispers.

Maybe it is. Maybe it isn't. It's impossible to say. All I know is that I couldn't have stopped what happened in here. It looks like a crime scene. The aftermath of a battle. All I heard was a noise in the hall, and when I opened my door, Gerard was standing there along with twenty people from Leo's security team. They wouldn't let me come down until it was over.

My sister smooths back her hair. Takes another deep breath. Her expression calms. Eva slides her coat off her shoulders and hands it to me. When she steps into the room, I follow her.

Eva approaches my brother slowly. Carefully. Leo doesn't look up at her. Neither does Haley. I don't know where she learned how to do this. How to just—walk into a room like this, where something has clearly gone wrong, where there is so much emotion in the air that it's hard to breathe. Eva kneels down in front of Leo and puts a hand on his shin.

His arms tighten around Haley. "She's not leaving," he says. "Ever."

"No," Eva answers. "But I think it's time to go upstairs."

"No one touches her." Leo still hasn't looked away from Haley. She runs her fingertips over his cheekbone. There's a bruise on her temple, getting darker by the second. Someone hit her. I doubt Leo will let that person live.

Eva pats his shin until he finally meets her eyes. "No one touches her," she promises.

"I'm tired," he says. My heart aches. I wonder if he knows he's crying. I don't think he does.

"I know. Go upstairs, and you can rest. Can you get up?"

Leo stands up like it's nothing. He has a cut on the side of his neck that he doesn't seem to notice. He's only concerned with Haley, who looks small, being carried like this. He goes toward the door, his eyes locked on her face, and Gerard ushers them out.

Eva picks up one of the turned-over chairs and sits in it. She puts her head in her hands. Lets out a deep breath.

"Is that what love looks like?" I just want to hear an answer. Any answer. From someone who knows more than me.

My sister laughs soundlessly behind her hands. "That's more than love," she says. "That's an obsession."

CHAPTER SEVENTEEN

Emerson

I'M JUST OUT of the shower and still cold from frozen surf when my phone lights up with an alert. Three alerts. I missed one of them when I was in the shower. Someone at the gate. Someone coming in. There's no video feed, because there are no cameras, only motion detectors. I am not interested in watching endless loops of video of the outside of my house. I am not interested in having myself captured on video. My blood pressure rises. Pulse goes up before I can grab it and pull it back down. I finish yanking my sweater over my head and snatch the phone from the shelf.

Alert: Front gate approach

Alert: Front gate entrance

Alert: Motion detected front door

I don't have a code on the gate itself. Will can't leave me the fuck alone about it. I'll never waste my breath trying to explain it. It's not as complicated as he pretends it is. Code systems are unreliable. On occasion, I need people to be able to get inside the gate without help from me.

Sinclair: Jesus Em open the door

He's out there with a duffel bag slung over one shoulder and the hood of his coat pulled up over a knit beanie. "The fuck is that?" I ask him. "You're not staying here."

"Hey, Emerson. Missed you so much." He slaps my shoulder on his way past me. Always barging in like this. The thousands of square feet around us contract. I lock the door while Sin opens my coat closet and hangs up his coat. He whips his hat off to reveal too-long dark hair. It's getting unruly.

"You need a haircut," I snap at him.

"Just a place to stay." He shuts the closet door and grins at me. "Luckily, my favorite brother has the space."

"Go camp on the beach. Or climb the bricks and sleep on the roof. Staying in a guest room is hardly adventurous." All Sin does is go on adventures. He's always scaling cliffs freehand or jumping out of planes and generally risking his life for no reason at all.

"Staying with you is always an adventure. Are

you going to offer me a drink?"

"I hate you."

"I love you too, Em."

We go through my office to the den behind it. No computers in sight in this room. Just leather furniture, a fireplace, and shelves full of books. One of Daphne's paintings hangs in the single display space. One of her smaller pieces, from college. It was early on in her study of the ocean. The brushwork and the colors are completely raw, almost like she attacked the canvas.

Sin stretches out in one of the leather chairs and searches around for the fireplace remote. He finds it, and the flames crackle to life in the grate. I open the cabinet on the mini bar. "Cold as hell out today. Did you surf?"

"What do you want to drink?"

"Vodka." He slings an arm behind his head and closes his eyes. "How cold is the water?"

"It's winter, Sin. It's fucking cold." I hold the glass in front of his face until he opens his eyes and takes it. I don't want a drink.

"Did you go out today?" He glances down at the vodka, then back up at me. "Other than to surf."

I don't want to sit with him, but looking down at him like this feels ridiculous. So I take the opposite seat. "Why are you here?"

"Answer me first."

Irritation makes my teeth snap together. Always with the questions. The endless questions, as if anything has changed. It never occurs to Sin that I don't want anything to be different.

Fine—I want one thing to be different. I want Daphne. There's nothing else I would change.

"Yeah. I walked for hours. I love long walks on the beach."

He narrows his eyes. Sips his vodka. "Is that sarcasm, or—"

"Jesus Christ."

My brother raises his free hand. "I'm only asking because—"

"Stop asking. Why are you here? Don't tell me it's for a goddamn family reunion." Will was talking about this on the phone. Getting the three of us back together.

"In a manner of speaking."

"You're kidding." My skin has gone cold beneath my clothes. Colder than it was when I climbed out of the ocean. Colder than when I let myself fall into the waves. "You're fucking kidding, Sin. You can't invite yourself into my house for a goddamn sleepover."

The way he puts the glass on the nearby table

is too deliberate. Firelight catches in the facets of the glass. Minuscule fires burn in the center of the diamonds. A cut of sunlight bisects the glass, throwing diamond rainbows onto the opposite wall. The light continues from the table to the rug to the bookshelves. Accents on the spines of the books gleam in that light. Metallic. Ordered. It would take another kind of brushstroke to replicate those bold bands.

"Emerson."

Sin's got his hands folded in front of him. I don't know how long I've been paying attention to the room. All I know is that it kept my heart from racing out of control.

"Tell me what you're doing here." He doesn't react to my tone, which is not polite, which is not kind at all. I don't know why he's here in my space. I'm finished playing games. He just watches me. It's worse than what Will does, which is to harass me until I want to kill him. Sin lets all his worry show on his face. "I can see what you're doing, prick. Tell me why you're here or get the fuck out of my house."

"I got a call from the prison." Sin looks me directly in the eyes as he says it. He's not in the sunlight. He is in shadow, which makes his eyes slightly more difficult to read. Eyes like mine.

Like our mother's. Other than this one feature, he looks like our father. All the light is behind him. The expression on his face, the tilt of his mouth—it's serious.

Hope feels like catching a wave. "Is he dead?"

He blows out a breath and looks down at his clasped hands. Back up at me. "Dad's up for parole."

Dust motes whirl softly through the air behind Sin's head. The wall behind him could be a still life featuring Daphne's painting. A round candle my housekeeper put underneath it. A small silver bowl that was given out at a charity event. There are angles at play in the light. Angles in the painting. They intersect and double back. Like a lattice. Like a pattern. Like light from around a closed door. A sliced-out rectangle on a bare floor. Sin, sitting in his chair. Waiting.

"I don't care."

"Yes, you do. We all care. You don't have to pretend it's not a big deal."

"I don't know why you think I'd have a problem with it."

He stares at me. "You do have a fucking problem with it. Why are you lying to me?"

"You could have told me this in a text."

Sin shakes his head slowly. "No, I don't think

I could have."

"Did you forget how to read? How to write?"

A frustrated, irritated grin spreads across his face. This grin is what makes him a minor Instagram celebrity. Women love to look at that shit. They don't know he only grins like that when he's pissed.

"I didn't forget anything, Emerson."

"This was a lovely visit." I stand up from my chair. Sin stands up, too. "Time for you to go."

"Not a chance in hell."

Anger and disappointment fight with each other. Going for blood. They're about to get loose. I thought that motherfucker might be dead. I'm a fucking fool. And I don't need Sin to see it. "Leave."

"No."

"I don't want you here."

"I don't care that much."

"What are you so afraid of?" I'm taunting him. Baiting him. Trying to back him toward the door, to get him the hell out of my house, but my brother stands his ground.

"Are you going to make me say it?" Sin laughs and sweeps his hand through the air, gesturing at me with my hands in my pockets. "You? Being like this? That's how I know everything is fucked."

"Oh? A person standing in his own den, waiting for his asshole brother to leave? That's how you know? It's how I know you should leave. I'm fine, and I don't give a fuck about Dad."

"I can see what you're doing, too." Fear is beating at the inside my chest now. An old, humiliating fear. It's cold, with long fingers that could pick a lock if it needed to. If it couldn't find another way out. "I see what you're doing, Emerson, I can see your face. You're making it into art."

I hate, *hate*, that Sin knows this about me. I hate that he knows how I keep the world at arm's length. By making it into a painting in my mind. By making it art. Considering it like art. At a frozen remove.

"Bold of you, to think you're art. You look like shit."

"You're not fine."

"I am."

"Bullshit."

"It's not."

"You should have taken a swing at me by now."

He's right. Emotions are a bell curve. On the one end, they're still lifes in black and white.

Motionless. Bolted to the wall. No need to react to anything. On the other end, they've come to life. Full color. A riot inside my head. The most control is necessary at those times, to keep myself in check. To keep them hidden. It takes all my attention to make the world into art. To freeze it in place. To make it into a representation of itself. A harmless commodity.

But in the middle, there's a space where I might let up on that iron grip. I might let myself fight with my brothers. Or punch Sin in his damn fool face.

"Get out." Light tone. Light light light. The opposite of the rocks weighing down my gut. The opposite of crushing disappointment. I thought he was dead, goddamn it.

"I'm staying. A few days, maybe the week."

"I have an event."

"Go to the event, then. I'll watch your house while you're gone."

"I'd like it better if you left. And if you never came back."

Sin presses his lips together and blinks. It hurt him, what I said, but I can't fathom why. I don't know why he wants this from me—this thing I can't give him. I'm never going to be able to give him the kind of brotherly bullshit he's looking for. Sin's wasting his time on me. He should concentrate on Will instead.

"Have you eaten lunch?" he asks.

"No." I don't tell him I wasn't going to eat lunch. That right now, I don't find food particularly interesting. The only thing I find interesting is Daphne. Her messages are infrequent. That makes me want them so much more.

Sin rubs his hands over his hair. "What's your favorite place to order in?"

"Any of them." I take my phone out of my pocket. I'm hungry for Daphne. Sin can't order her for delivery. "I don't care."

Emerson: I want to know what you taste like, little painter.

"Could you fake it, then?"

I meet Sin's eyes. I don't like what I find there. Genuine concern. The last thing I need is for him to insist on staying past this week. The last thing I need is for him to interfere in my plans. And if he gets worried enough, he will.

My phone goes back into my pocket. "La Table. If Marie answers the phone, she prefers you order in French."

Sin rolls his eyes. "Jesus Christ."

"My apologies. Should I have pretended to

care a little less?" I actually do like La Table. But now that I've sent that message to Daphne, all my nerves have kicked into overdrive. If she would tell me where she was…

I can't leave.

I would take her. Spirit her away. Take her far from whatever nonsense is keeping her from me. I would spread her sweet thighs and find out how my little painter tastes.

My heart pounds. I'll have to do something soon, because living like this—it's not tenable for anyone, but least of all me. I can be very, very patient. I will be so fucking patient with her.

I won't wait forever.

I can't wait that long.

"The fuck are you thinking about?" Sin asks. He has his phone to his ear. "Are you imagining murder? That's what it looks like."

I need to send a message. One to my man in the city.

Emerson: Confirm her location by the end of the evening.

Daphne has four brothers. She still hasn't told me which one she's staying with. I have my suspicions. I need to know for sure.

Fine—two messages.

Emerson: And a way in.

"No." This time, I'm going to tell him the truth. "Something much nicer than that."

CHAPTER EIGHTEEN

Emerson

EVERY YEAR, I am invited to a certain charity gala in the city. It's part dinner, part art auction. The proceeds go to funding fine arts classes for disadvantaged children in Manhattan and the surrounding boroughs. Every year, I send a significant donation along with my regrets.

Not this year.

My little painter is the keynote speaker. She's one of the guests of honor. Her attendance has been confirmed by three separate news outlets in the past week.

Convenient, because there is no way into her brother's house. He lives outside the city in a fortress. It's crawling with security. I don't know whether he's always this cautious. Perhaps he's heard about me. Perhaps there are other rivalries at work. That's where Daphne is being kept.

Logan lets me out onto the sidewalk into a barrage of camera flashes. The afterimages of snowflakes imprint on my vision. Cold tests the edges of my jacket. I don't stay long enough to let it in. Up the sidewalk between rows of manicured evergreen hedges. Up the stairs to the venue. In through the front doors.

It was a private residence at one time, but now it's a sought-after event space in the city. Crown moldings as far as the eye can see, and white walls to provide a neutral backdrop to jewel-toned dresses and black tuxedos. They've torn out most of the interior walls on the main level. A girl in black takes my coat and hands me a ticket.

It's time to find her.

I ignore the nagging urge to focus on the details of the room. It makes it more tolerable to be in spaces like this. In crowds like this. I replace it with the hunt for my little painter. It's been too long since I touched her.

"Emerson." An older man steps into my path, holding out his hand. Alfie Chambers is red-cheeked and jovial as hell. He has a firm grip. "I didn't think I'd see you here. What brought you out? Margery. Say hello to Emerson." His wife, who has never uttered an audible word in my presence, steps graciously to his side. Alfie doesn't wait for her to say anything. "The pieces up for auction. Which one's yours?"

"I haven't decided yet." Daphne's. I haven't

seen it yet, but I know the others will pale in comparison.

"Leave something for the rest of us, would you?" He spots someone else over my shoulder and blessedly leaves the conversation.

I don't see her. I know what I'm looking for. Her soft, shining hair, so dark it's almost black. Her eyes. The shape of her waist. I'm looking for them in a hundred sweeps of expensive fabric.

Not here. Not here. Not here.

Hunting for her takes on the guise of making the rounds. My presence is causing a bit of a stir. Whichever piece I decide to buy in the auction will shoot up in value as soon as I've made the purchase. The artist will be remarked upon.

Daphne will be remarked upon.

I don't like that. I don't want anyone else looking at her, or talking about her.

The long gallery where the auction pieces are being displayed is busy. Couples walk arm in arm in front of the pieces. Each one has its own attendant taking bids for the silent auction.

No Daphne, but her work is here. It's among five other pieces. I pass by the one by Peter Clay with only a cursory glance. A second piece makes no impression. And then there is Daphne's.

It stops my heart.

It's not like the other pieces she's done. Other pieces I've bought. I own almost all of her available work. Everything that's been listed online, either by her former college or by Motif.

The ocean fills the entire canvas. Dark seas, no sky. She usually paints the surface, with at least a hint of the horizon. Not this time. This is the deep, and it's not peaceful. Red slashes cut through deepest blue. A victim has been dragged through the current in the mouth of a predator. There are too many slashes for survival to be possible, yet she hasn't shown the moment of attack. The horror is hidden out of frame, but the aftermath hangs in the sea.

I step closer to read the small plaque with the title of the piece.

Blood in the Water.

Jesus Christ.

I knew she was hiding something. All those dark waves—how could she not be? *It's in my head. It's all that ends up on the canvas.* She was talking about the ocean. Her secrets. I never imagined they would look like this. My heart races. Her wide, dark eyes are too innocent for a scene like this.

Or perhaps they're not.

Need cuts into me like the crimson slashes on

the canvas. In this case, her art obscures. Whatever this is, I want to hear it from her. Drag it out of her body in tears and shudders. *At first it was some commentary about how the water hides things, and how it's never the same twice.* No. Her painting is what hides her. Daphne's art reveals only the surface, but it pretends it's telling you everything. I discover both hands are over my mouth and put them back into my pockets.

"This piece is mine," I tell the attendant for Daphne's piece. He leans in, his expression neutral. "I'm buying it under my corporation." The name I give him is an anonymous shell. I don't care if this painting skyrockets in value—Daphne is priceless. What I care about is buying myself some time. This piece is too personal to announce I've bought it without some consideration. "Anyone meets my bid, raise it by five thousand dollars. It's mine at the end of the night. Do you understand?"

"I do, Mr. Leblanc." He understands enough to stand perfectly still while I tuck a thousand dollars into the front pocket of his suit jacket.

"Emerson," someone says. They're circling now. Waiting to see which pieces I pay attention to.

"No."

I don't stop to see whether they're taken aback or not. I want her in my sight. All the cryptic text messages. The worried tone seeping through the words on the screen. This painting.

Daphne Morelli is not all right.

All my attention goes to finding her. She is the guest of honor at this event. She'll be where the important people are. The richest bastards among us. My head aches from staying aware of all the people in the space while I look for her. It's the worst of all worlds. The renovations have made the carved-out rooms too large, but they're still too crowded.

I find her in a ritzy gathering in front of a low stage that won't be used until it's time to announce the winners of the silent auction.

I find her with a man.

A boy, my mind supplies. A fucking boy. Someone who has recently graduated, if I were to guess.

Someone who has his hands on my little painter.

They're standing near a clutch of people, none of whom seem to notice that Daphne doesn't want to be touched.

He turns his head, and I recognize him. Peter Clay. My mind lights up with the memory of

Daphne's face as she described his work. A flat expression. Narrowed eyes. She doesn't like him. Doesn't want to be near him.

But he's leaning in, one hand on her waist, and as I approach them, he pulls her closer to his body.

And she—

Resists.

It's as subtle as I would have expected. A stiffness in her shoulders. A slight turn of her face away from his. Her dark eyes blank. Distant. It makes my blood roar in my ears. My hatred for this unbelievable fuck is spilling out of the canvas, breaking free. It's only countered by an intense awareness of how many other people are in the room. It's impossible to know what they'll do if I react the way I want to, which is to kill him.

Too many people in the space. Too many witnesses. And Daphne. Calculations sprint through my mind. They lay themselves over the fury simmering in my blood. They try to hold it back. Hold it down. I want to hurt Peter Clay. I won't do it where Daphne can see. I won't do it where anyone else can see her and draw their own conclusions. About my little painter. About me. Fifteen feet away. Ten feet. Five. His hand is still at her waist.

My skin is on fire with the need to touch her. I take his hand instead. Wrench it away from her body and into mine.

"Peter Clay." I turn my grip into a crushing handshake and push him away from her. Anger flashes in his eyes, but then they widen with surprise. "I've heard so much about you."

"Mr. Leblanc." He twists his hand out of mine and manages not to rub at it. "You're the famous one. I didn't know you'd be here tonight." It's been five seconds, and he's already forgotten about Daphne. His dull gray eyes glint with opportunity. Greed. "Did you happen to see the pieces in the gallery? I was hoping to get your opinion on mine."

It was garbage, I bite back. I can't stand in this crowd for ten minutes without everyone watching. It's a fine line, now. Too much longer and they'll assume I give a fuck about him. They'll all assume his paintings are worth something. "I've seen them. But now isn't the place to discuss work like that. Where is your studio?"

He sticks his hands in his pockets and feigns nonchalance. "I have a space above Worth-Kelley in Chelsea. I'm there most weekdays, if you—"

"Tomorrow afternoon," I announce. "I only attend private showings."

Peter Clay's eyebrows go up. This is more than he ever could have hoped for. "I'm sure we can accommodate that."

We. As if he owns the gallery. He doesn't. "Tell them I'll be there at two."

"Of course." His eyes dart back behind. "Of course I'll do that. It was a pleasure to meet you, Mr. Leblanc."

"Don't let me take any more of your time."

Peter Clay has the good sense to edge away for several feet before he turns and rushes into the crowd. And I turn back to the only person worth anything.

Daphne stands with her back straight and her hands clasped in front of her, as gorgeous as I've ever seen her in a dark blue gown that matches the color scheme of her painting. Delicate tendrils of her hair frame her face. The rest has been swept back in an elegant twist and dotted with pearls. For a person who's standing so still, she's breathing fast, her shoulders rising and falling above the gown's neckline. Her makeup is dark and rich, making her look older than she is. I can see through it. I can see how young, and innocent, and fucking pure she is, and how dare he touch her.

How dare he.

Red lips part. "I didn't know you were coming."

"I had a piece to bid on."

"Mine?"

"Who else's?"

The corner of her mouth curves up ruefully. "Peter's, maybe. Everyone else is very excited about it."

Daphne's smile fades away too soon. Her makeup is beautiful. Professional. But it doesn't hide everything about her skin. She looks pale. Is it from that motherfucker, or whatever happened to inspire her painting?

I step closer and bend to speak into her ear. "I don't give a fuck about his painting. I give a fuck that he had his hands on you."

She gives a nervous laugh. "That's how he is. He's over the top and pushy. He would have let go eventually."

He'll never touch her again. That's how this will play out. But I don't say this to Daphne. There's something far more pressing to talk about.

"I saw your painting," I murmur into the shell of her ear. "What's wrong?"

"Nothing." Her voice quavers. She's close enough that I can feel the rest of her shaking along with it. The air around her trembles.

"Do you need to leave?" I'll take her in my arms and carry her out now, if she says the word. Let these people speculate.

"I can't," she breathes. "I have to give a speech. And my security will be looking for me. I can't leave with you."

She can't stay here. There are tears in her voice. I won't have her breaking down in front of all these people. "When is the speech?"

"In an hour."

"And do they follow you into the ladies' room?"

"No." She blushes. "Of course not."

"Then take a walk with me."

"I can't."

"Inside." Daphne hesitates. "I know a place with no prying eyes, little painter. You'll be safe there. Walk with me."

More hesitation. My heart twists itself up. I want her out of this goddamn room. I want her in my arms. Patience is excruciating. Daphne tips her head up to look into my eyes. "I have to be back for the speech," she says softly.

"I won't steal you away," I promise.

I won't steal her yet.

"Okay." Daphne threads her arm through mine. "Yes. Please. Let's go somewhere else."

Chapter Nineteen

Daphne

KNOW I shouldn't go with him. It's one of the most basic rules of staying alive. You don't follow a man down a dark hallway without telling other people. My heart beats fast, up near my throat. Leo sent his favorite driver, Thomas, with me tonight. I made him stay at the edge of the ballroom. I didn't want to be watched. I didn't want someone hovering while I shook hands and tried to do art-world networking.

I regretted *that* the instant Peter Clay leaned in to proposition me.

I'm not sure I regret it now.

"I haven't painted you yet, Daphne," Peter cooed into my ear. "People would go crazy for that piece. I'd make you look incredible."

There's no way on the planet I'll ever get naked and cry for Peter Clay. I wanted to push him away. I wanted to slap him for putting his hand on my waist like he had any right. But old instincts kicked in and I did nothing. It's safer to do nothing. To be nothing. But it feels like shit.

I'm not paying attention to where Emerson is taking me. Through the main room of this renovation. A door. Hallway. I check over my shoulder to make sure Thomas isn't following. Another door. He makes a turn into a corner that's pure shadow and dark and opens yet another door. Ushers me through. I come back to myself when the door closes behind me with a firm click.

He locks it.

We're in a closet. A storage area. White fabric drapes over tables and chairs. Faint golden light comes in from outside. Christmas lights from the garden outside. Emerson's hand makes gentle contact with the small of my back. I shouldn't trust him. Shouldn't let myself be locked in this room with him. My heart feels like a ticking clock. How long do I have before Thomas finds me?

Emerson moves in front of me, skimming his fingers over the place Peter touched me. His eyes take my breath away, even in this soft light. Everything about him is perfect. Perfect dark suit. Perfect fall of sandy hair. He touches my wrist next, then runs his fingers up my arm, his eyes on my face. I thought I was holding it together out there. I thought I was hiding it pretty well. Now I feel unsteady in my heels. All my muscles are tired from standing, and I haven't been standing very long. Waves of heat and cold go down the back of my neck.

"You can tell me, little painter." His palm is on my cheek. He has big, strong hands, and a lean, solid body. I try to breathe normally. Fail.

"I'm fine," I lie. "It was too warm in there. Peter was—" Disgusting. "I don't like him, but I didn't want to make a scene."

"What else?"

"There's nothing else."

"I saw your painting," he says again, a glimmer of emotion in his voice. "I know there's something else."

His touch feels more possessive now. A harder grip. My heart goes into overdrive. The door is locked.

And.

My chest aches with how much I want to tell him. It's dangerous to tell secrets. It's dangerous to reveal anything. And Emerson was so quietly furious when he pushed Peter away from me. I can still feel that intensity in his touch. It's slowly filling up the room. I could drown in it. The pressure's too much to stay quiet.

"It's my brother."

Emerson's eyes narrow. There's an instant charge in the air, like the hum before a lightning strike. "Did he hurt you?"

"No. Jesus. Why would you say that?" I don't realize I'm pulling away until I feel the pressure of his hand holding me in place.

His thumb skims over my cheekbone, his eyes fiercer now. Brows drawn together. "Because you sound terrified. Because you won't answer my texts. Because you keep saying you can't leave. Don't do that."

"Don't do what?"

"Don't hide your face." It's an easy command. Him to me. I was doing it without knowing. I look back at him, defensiveness scraping at my insides along with a conflicting urge to obey.

"Leo would never hurt me." A memory flashes into my mind. Looking over Leo's shoulder while he took the stairs to the second floor two at a time. He was carrying me in his arms. I was small, then. Small enough to be afraid without knowing exactly why. It's a very old memory, fragmented and short. His hands on a pile of CDs next to my pink CD player, slipping headphones over my ears. *Listen to the whole CD and tell me which is your favorite. Don't you want to listen? I'll be right back.* "Don't ever say that. I'm worried about him. That's what I meant."

Emerson looks into my eyes like he can see what I'm not saying. "Is he sick?"

"He was."

"Like cancer?"

"No. He's okay now." I can feel myself backing away from the topic. Morellis don't tell family secrets to other people. I'm running up against a firm boundary. I cannot tell Emerson that Leo was shot. I can't tell him he almost died twice. I can't tell him about the chalk-pale color of Leo's face after Haley left. All of it's hitting me now, like it did in the car on the way over. "But I was—I was living with him, and I saw how bad things could get. I'm worried something else will happen to him. All I want—" I wish I could breathe normally. Keep it cool. But I can't. "All I want is to be independent, but I can't. Not with my family. I don't want to leave them behind, or cut myself off—I couldn't do that. But I'm scared," I admit. "I'm scared. I can feel how weak it makes me."

"You're brave, little painter. Not weak."

I let out an unsteady laugh. "You don't know that. I bet you're Mr. Independent."

Emerson sobers. "My brother came to visit me

this week, and I was an asshole. I pushed him away. Told him he should leave, and never come back. But that's not strength. Strength is what you do for your family."

"You have a brother?" I don't know why I find it so surprising. Maybe it's just that Emerson seems so solitary.

"I have two brothers."

"I'm sure you do more for them than I do for my family. I don't do anything."

He taps his fingers on my chest, over my heart. "The worrying, and caring—you love them. That's what you do for them."

"You don't worry about your brothers?"

"No." The way he says it sounds like a lie. "I'm not like you."

"Maybe you're better off that way." My voice cracks on the last word, because I mean it. I really, really do. Maybe it would be better if I was strong and independent and not just someone to worry about. Maybe it would be better if Leo had never had to carry me upstairs away from our rampaging father. Maybe it all would have been better.

"I'm not." Emerson's arms fold around me. I would cry if it weren't for the strong embrace. His hard chest under expensive clothes.

A cage, I think, and sensation lights up all

down my spine. It feels good. It feels good to be trapped here by him. It feels good to be held in place. I search out his jacket with my hands and hold on. I can feel his heartbeat. Fast. Understanding crashes into my mind. He's tense. Holding me and holding back. Emerson's arms tighten and I suck in a little breath. I couldn't get free now. Couldn't pull myself away.

"Stop me," he mutters.

"What?"

He takes my face in his hand and tilts it up. Those blue-green eyes are all shadows now. "Stop me," he says again.

I shake my head.

And then his mouth is on mine, aggressive and searching and hot. Nothing like it was in the gallery. That was gentle, I see now. An overture. Now he's powerful verging on rough. Teeth sink into my lip like he can't resist biting me. Just enough to hurt me. Just enough to make me gasp, and press against him. Emerson takes my breath away, kissing it out of me, not letting me have more air. I know I should pull away, but I don't want to. I push into him instead. Kiss him back as hard as he's kissing me. Embarrassment flickers across the back of my mind. I haven't done this, I'm not good at this, but I am compelled. I want this dangerous man closer and I tug wildly on his jacket. He's already as close as he can get.

I bite him back.

Emerson hisses. "You think it's weak, how much you give, how far you bend, but it's not. Look at how much I need you." He takes my hand from his jacket and pushes it down to the front of his pants. He's hard and huge underneath the expensive fabric. "You're holding all the fucking power."

I can't speak. Can't breathe. Can only shake my head. No. I don't have any power. I've never dreamed of power. My family is powerful, and I am safe. That's all I've ever thought about.

"I'll make you believe me."

He lifts me by the waist like I'm weightless, and I don't even have time to gasp before he perches me on one of the tables. My dress crumples in his fist. Oh, Jesus, I can't go back out there in a ruined gown. Everyone would see. Everyone would know. But Emerson doesn't rip it. He pushes it up to my waist.

Emerson looks down at my naked thighs, breathing hard, and when his eyes meet mine again, a shock goes through me. I've never seen this in a man's eyes before. Desire like this. It's dark, and terrifying, and I want it.

He gets to his knees in front of the table. *The dust*, I want to say. His beautiful, expensive suit. Warm palms meet my knees, and he opens my legs.

A moment of sheer terror engulfs me and I scramble for his wrists, try to close my legs at the same time. He won't let me do it. He's stronger, even on his knees, and he arches a disapproving eyebrow at me. Shame heats my face.

"No one," I say, breathless, my voice thin. "No one's ever seen me like this."

I've never seen a more feral grin. It's only a flicker, gone in a heartbeat, but that single moment is enough to make my face combust. Emerson plucks one of my hands from his wrist and puts it on his shoulder. Then the other. "I'm going to do more than look."

His hands glide up to my inner thighs and he pushes them apart with even pressure. One hand stays in place to hold me open. He can't see anything yet. I have panties on. Lacy, but they still exist. Emerson runs the pad of his thumb over the placket. Good thing I'm holding on to his shoulders. I would collapse otherwise. Crumple to the ground from the sheer sensation.

"Wet," he comments. "Show me the rest. You can move one of your hands to do it."

"Oh my god," I whisper. But my hand is already moving between my legs. It's shaking so much I can barely hook a finger into the fabric, but I do it. I pull it to the side. The panties aren't made for this and it's an uncomfortable stretch, pulling at all the seams against my skin.

Emerson looks.

He puts his thumb idly to his mouth and licks me off of it. "Fuck," he murmurs. "Look at you. Look at this pussy. It's fucking gorgeous. Is it bare for me?"

"I didn't know you would be here."

"That's not what I asked."

I'm going to die of embarrassment. "It's not for you."

"Liar." With a curse, he knocks my hand away and grips the lace in his fist. The ripping sound is louder than my heartbeat, louder than my breath. Emerson's hands go to the crease of my thighs and I grab at his jacket to keep myself from falling. His thumbs run over my softest skin. "Jesus," he says, and then he adds a pressure that opens my folds, exposing them to the air and the burn of his eyes. His breath is hot on my skin. "You smell so fucking good."

Part of my fear drops away, but it's replaced by another wave of shame that he's so close like this, looking so intently, seeing everything.

"I need it," he murmurs, almost to himself, and then his mouth is between my legs.

It's so intense that I arch away, try to run. He grips my ass and pins me to the edge of the table. My mind is nothing. I'll never think again. I'll never paint again. I'll be an explosion of pleasure, like fireworks in my brain. I can't breathe. Getting lightheaded. The flat of his tongue is replaced with the tip, circling my opening, lapping at it like he'll never get enough.

It feels so good. I don't know how to do this. I try to spread my legs wider and move my hips into him. It's dirty, doing this, it's not right to do this in a closet at a charity gala. My fingers dig into his jacket. Oh, Jesus, it's good. My mind careens between his tongue and my shame. Spreading my legs for a man in a supply closet. Letting him lick me, and taste me. Not stopping him.

He makes a sound against my pussy like I am the best thing he's ever had in his mouth, ever ever ever, and then he focuses his attention on my clit. My vision blurs. I'm going to fall off the table, except I can't. He's holding me here.

"I can't do this," I pant. "I've never—I've never—"

"Come on my tongue, little painter."

"Wait. Wait—"

He doesn't wait. He does something magical with his tongue, something wicked, and pleasure tears into me like a bomb. It looks golden. My vision goes dark, tinged in gold. It looks golden, to have my breath stolen like this. It takes all my self-control away from me and rocks my hips and makes muscles I've never felt before clench and flutter. Emerson doesn't stop. He keeps going and going and going and I reach the peak of this pleasure and meet another one. My despair comes out in a moan—god, no, I can't let him do this, I'm already doing this—and his answering hum of approval is more than I can bear.

And it's not over. He keeps tasting me until the last shivers have wrung themselves out, until I can see again. Until I take a full breath, then another. One last, long lick. My fingers are cramped from holding his jacket. Emerson stands, pressing the sleeve of his jacket to his mouth. His eyes gleam. I've never seen him rumpled like this. I made wrinkles in his suit, and his knees are dusty from the floor. His eyes drop down to where I'm still open for him.

He holds out his hand.

I take it.

Emerson helps my dress fall back to the floor. He swipes a thumb at the corner of my mouth. My heart thunders. If he were going to steal me, if he were going to take me, he could do it now. No one would notice for a while yet.

"The color's back in your cheeks," he says, voice low. "Let's take you back to the gala."

CHAPTER TWENTY

Emerson

THE NEXT MORNING, I lean into the guest room and find my brother on his laptop. "Time to go."

Sin cuts a look at me with suspicion in his eyes. "I've only been here a couple days."

"And what did I do? I attended a goddamn charity gala. I'm fine. Get out of my house."

The truth is, I need him gone. I cannot stop thinking about Daphne. The need to be with her is so strong it feels like a drug. She tasted so good I'm still reeling from it. The demand for more is on an animal level. Sin's presence competes with it in the most obnoxious way. I can't be calm when he's here, and I'm thinking of her so much I'm losing bits of time. Five minutes here. Ten minutes there. I refuse to answer any questions about it. Sin won't accept that it's just planning, and then he'll insist on staying, and fuck that.

He looks me up and down. "Are you going into the city?"

"I have a meeting. Be gone when I come back."

"Fine." His fingers tap on the keyboard. "But I'm staying close. I'm getting a hotel."

"Good. Great to see you."

Sin rolls his eyes. "If you thought it was so great, you'd tell me a hotel isn't necessary."

"Is it better if I said I wish you hadn't come?"

He glares at me. "No."

"Then it was great to see you."

Logan drives me into the city and lets me out the customary fifteen blocks away. Wind whips in from the side, chilling the back of my neck over my coat. It was hell on the water this morning. Sin is such a fucking busybody. I don't know what more he wants from me. I surf. I walk fifteen blocks to almost every destination. I force myself to be outside, even though on days like today it feels like having my skull in a vise. A block goes by, and it's still difficult to breathe.

Iron clouds hang over the city. Fat snowflakes spiral lazily toward the concrete. They're like pinpricks of light against the washed-out backdrop. Black pavement tire tracks gleam in the center of the street. A woman's red coat sways from side to side like a bell. Her shadow moves this way and that. The harder I focus, the easier it is to inhale.

I still hate it out here.

The Worth-Kelley building is a modern three-story wedged between a museum and an office building. It's the opposite of Motif in every possible way, from the gleaming white I to the oversized windows on each floor. I stroll in through the front door. The hardwood here shines, and the air is lightly scented with a hint of something clean and bright. Lemon, maybe. A secretary waits at a desk by the door. She's a display piece as much as the art. Perfect makeup. Sleek hair. A low-cut top.

One glance at me, and her eyes widen. "Hello, Mr. Leblanc," she says. "We're so happy to welcome you to Worth-Kelley. Can I get you anything? A drink? Sparkling water?"

"No." I take one glove off, then the next. "I'm here for a private showing." I give the space a cursory glance. She seizes the moment and reaches for something below the lip of the desk. Her hands fly over it. A surreptitious text, no doubt.

"Yes. Of course." She shows off a row of white, perfect teeth. "There's no one in the second-floor gallery or the studios upstairs. Peter made sure of it."

Peter Clay himself ambles down the stairs to

the left. He watches where he's going. When he arrives at the bottom, he runs a hand over his hair.

"Melanie, can you—oh, hi." His eyebrows go up in perhaps the worst approximation of surprise I've ever seen. "The famous collector. Welcome to my humble abode. Mel, I was just going to ask if you could give the mayor's office a call."

"About the piece?"

"That's the one." My god, I hate him. "Thanks. Mr. Leblanc, all my work is on the second floor. Easier to keep them all in one place. We could talk while you look. I don't want to make any assumptions, but if it was a commission you're looking for…"

He leads me up the stairs, talking and talking. The second floor of the gallery is indeed full of Peter Clay pieces. He's been busy. There are at least twenty in here, but the room has been divided. Carve-outs and alcoves and corners. It's clearly meant to provide a visual barrier between the works of different artists. Worth-Kelley is betting that he's as special as they think he is.

"This one." I point to a random painting. "Tell me about your technique." Off he goes. Either Peter Clay doesn't hear the boredom in my voice, or he's doing a masterful job ignoring it. We reach the next painting. "An interesting decision," I say.

"What's that?"

"You've all but hidden the shadows. Your model is nearly part of the background."

"Oh, yes. I thought the interplay of—"

You thought you were making art, but you were wasting good paint and canvas. The next painting. The next. The next. I cut abruptly to the other side of the gallery. Peter jogs to keep up.

"You're left-handed," I say.

This cuts off his stream-of-consciousness nonsense. "How did you know that?"

"The brushstrokes."

It's bullshit. I know because he told me, the fucking fool. He gives everything away. Peter feels very safe in here. Very secure.

I turn away from this painting and turn a corner.

Peter hurries to stand next to me. "This is one of my favorite pieces. I'm looking for the perfect home, because I can't let it go for—" He's weak. Unsuspecting. I slam him face-first into the painting. Not hard enough to crack his nose, unfortunately. "Shit, man. Jesus. What the hell?"

I have him by the neck, his left arm twisted behind his back. Pent-up fury is an ache in my bones. I'd like to remove the light in his eyes, but no—no. The security cameras at the front of the room can't see this space, but the secretary saw me. Poor girl shouldn't have to discover a dead body.

Peter wriggles, but he can't get free. His cheek is shoved hard against an enormous painting of a girl with tears swimming in her eyes. I would guess she's eighteen. He's captured the self-conscious tilt of her shoulders. Unlike some of the other pieces, this one shows her full body. Her posture, and the set of her feet, give the sense that she's in the act of turning away.

"You can have all the paintings," Peter says. "Let's just—let me up so we can—"

"You're never going to speak to Daphne Morelli again," I say. "You're never going to look at her. You won't so much as fucking think about her."

"What?" His eyes bug out with his shock. "What did she tell you? I never touched her. She wanted it."

I let his words hang in the air until he realizes his mistake.

"We're friends," he tries again. "I only wanted her to model for me."

Anger breaks free. Only wanted her to model for him—fuck that. "You wanted her to model for you?"

"Yes," he chokes. "She's beautiful. Of course I wanted to paint her."

"You use a reference, don't you?"

"Like most painters." He has no fucking idea where I'm going with this. In the spirit of honesty, it's getting away from me a little. I force down the need to cede control to my rage. I will not beat the shit out of him, leaving him bruised and bloody. Not today.

"So the women come to your studio, ready to be painted, and then you make them take off their clothes—"

"They agree," he insists. "They're in agreement."

"And you take the reference photos."

"Yeah."

"How do you make them cry?"

His mouth drops open, his visible eye going even wider, and the depth of my hatred expands until it could swallow this pathetic gallery whole. I didn't plan to say any of this to him. This fucker is still grasping for an answer. If he was smart, if he could lie to save himself, he'd have said *I don't. Of course I don't. I add that later. Artistic license.*

But he is not smart, and he cannot lie, and I tighten my grip on the back of his neck.

I want to snap it. I let go of his arm and Peter flinches. He thinks I'm going to punch him. He'd deserve it. He deserves to have his skull cracked while all these weeping girls watch from their frames.

I put my fingertips on the canvas near his face instead. Trace the thick paint lines there, over her cheek. "How much do you get paid?"

He swallows. "It—it depends on the piece."

"Every time you use that brush. How much would you say every stroke was worth?" Peter doesn't know whether to answer this musing tone, so he keeps his mouth shut. "Oh, it's quite a bit, isn't it? *American Art Collector* called you a modern-day Rembrandt, but I don't think so."

Peter Clay is frozen in fear, so much so that he doesn't bother to hide his arms. I wrench the left one back behind him and bend his wrist. His fingers. Tighter and tighter and tighter. He clenches his jaw, his face going red, and tries to relieve some of the pressure by turning his body.

"How much would they like your paintings if I break your fingers?"

I'm on the edge. On the verge. If I squeeze much harder, his fingers will break. I've already done some damage to his wrist. He's gone limp with the shock.

I give him a shake. "How much, Peter?"

"I can't paint right-handed," he bursts out. "Don't do this. Don't do this, man. I didn't hurt her."

"And now you never will."

"I'll leave her alone. I promise." Oops. I did squeeze harder. Peter lets out a strangled groan. Probably a sprain. He'll have to take a little time off. He'll have to keep his mouth shut, if he doesn't want me to ruin him completely. It's so tempting. "I promise," he says again.

I squeeze a little bit harder. Too close. Too close to the edge. I pull Peter's head back from the painting and drive it into the wall again.

And then I let go.

He cowers against the painting. I pace back a few steps and pull my gloves out of my pocket. One goes on, then the next. I put all my emotions back where they belong. Silent. Still. Ordered. A whisper of concern crosses my mind. It's more difficult to control myself when it comes to Daphne. Worse yet, she makes me want to feel things. Well—*want* is a strong word. She makes me curious about what it would be like to stop shoving my feelings away.

Peter can't hide any longer. He turns away from the wall, holding his wrist with the other hand. In addition to being a fucking coward, a fucking piece of shit, he's pissed himself. The painting behind him is ruined.

"I think that's enough for today," I announce. "I won't be making a purchase."

I leave him standing there. I'm in the middle of the gallery when he calls after me.

"You're not going to say anything," he says.

About him. This little worm is terrified I'll walk outside and start talking. He knows as well as I do that it would only take a phone call or two, and Peter Clay would disappear from the art world. A few people might remember his name, but most of them would follow my lead. He'd never sell another painting.

"It would be best if you never brought yourself to my attention again."

Peter Clay has no further questions.

Chapter Twenty-One

Daphne

THE TEXT COMES in just as I'm picking up my phone after Leo's wedding.

Emerson: Come with me.

Daphne: I can't! I'm not in the city!!

It's a lie, of course. I am in the city. Leo wanted to get married in his own church, and so he did. I didn't know he still went to church. Any church, much less this one in the city.

Eva knows. He told me.

And for the first time, I got to watch how a secret hides in plain sight.

He simply announced that he's getting married at this church, on this date, and refused to say anything else about it. He let people assume what they wanted. What they assume is that Leo is a Morelli son who only got married in the church to please his parents. They don't know that my father complained bitterly about the location up until he got out of the car this morning.

They don't know anything, really.

Emerson's reply comes right away.

Emerson: I know where you are, little painter.

Emerson: You're in the basement of St. Thomas's church as we speak. Come to the sacristy.

My entire body heats, then freezes. He knew I was lying. He knows I'm here.

He could be here, too. Is he?

I've thought of him every day since the charity gala. Every minute.

At first, I tried not to answer his texts. There was Christmas, and wedding planning, and as much painting as I could fit in. But I couldn't help myself. I texted him back.

I tried not to think of his mouth on my pussy. I tried so hard. The most important thing was to keep the peace with my brother, and help Haley, and be there for Eva. No matter what I wanted. No matter what bad, dangerous things I wanted to do.

If he's here—

I run up the stairs to the main floor of the church before I can think about it anymore. If he's here—if he takes me—

I burst into the sacristy and my heart sinks.

He's not here.

There is only a single, white orchid in the middle of the table. He was close. He was in this room while I stood up in Leo's wedding. He might have been watching me. Goose bumps run up and down my arms. I lift the flower from the table to feel one of the petals.

This is as close as Emerson has come to me since the gala.

Unless he's been closer, and I didn't know.

Emerson's obsession is palpable. In the delicate stem of the flower. In the close air of the sacristy. He came into this church while my entire family was inside. That act alone is dangerous. How did he do it, I wonder? Pretend to be a guest? Or was he a shadow who came through a door while no one was looking?

"Daphne?" My sister's voice echoes into the sacristy. "Where are you? The cars are leaving."

I whirl around and shove the white orchid into my bridesmaids bouquet. A second later, Eva comes into view. She looks gorgeous in her silk dress. All of the bridesmaids wear custom designs. Eva's idea, Leo's money. I could wear mine again.

"Oh, there you are. What are you doing back here? Are you okay?"

"Just needed a second to breathe."

And maybe run away. Maybe run straight into Emerson's car. My blood is still hot with the idea of him in this church during Leo's wedding. He was here. He left the orchid as proof. As a gift for me to find. It's both sweet and terrifying.

"Your face is red." Eva steps closer to smooth a tendril of hair behind my ear. "You sure you're all right? Leo won't mind if you hang out upstairs during the reception."

"No way. There's going to be champagne and dancing. I'm good, really. I think maybe I locked my knees during the ceremony."

"Okay. Come ride with me?"

We step out of the church together a minute later. Cars line the sidewalk in front of the church. I try to find Emerson's. I don't see it, but I know he's here. He asked me to come with him. Eva's standing at one of the black SUVs, waving me forward.

"Come on," she says, laughing. "I'm freezing."

No more texts from Emerson. He'll know by now that I left. I want to be at the reception. Leo's my first brother to get married, and I don't want to miss it.

It's crazy to trust Emerson. It's dangerous to want him.

Answering him at all is a risk.

But every time his name appears on my phone screen, my heart does something strange and good, like it's trying to get out of my body and go to him. I know how it sounds. It sounds like I'm out of my mind. Snow comes down outside the window as we speed out of the city and onto the highway.

"What's on your mind?" Eva's mind is on her phone. She's texting continuously, her thumbs flying over the screen of her phone.

"Is something going wrong at the house? Who are you texting?"

"The coordinator. I'm letting her know that Leo and Haley are five minutes ahead of us. The servers only have a couple minutes to get ready after they arrive." She glances over at me. "But you're staring out the window and mooning over something."

"I'm not mooning."

Wishing, maybe. Wishing I'd been braver and gone out to Emerson. Let him take me away. But being brave in this case also means being an asshole. Disappearing in the middle of Leo's wedding day would ruin it, no question.

"Daphne."

"Eva."

"Don't lie," she sings. "I can see you staring out the window."

I stare at her with huge eyes until she laughs. "You already planned this entire reception. Let the coordinator do her job."

"You're right, you're right." She drops her phone into her purse and leans her head back on the seat. "Dad is in rare form today."

"I've never seen anyone more pissed off at a wedding. He was, like, glowering the entire ceremony."

"He looked sick with jealousy," Eva muses.

"Like Dad would ever want to marry a Constantine."

Eva huffs. "Probably not."

Who the hell knows, though? I never in my life thought Leo would marry a Constantine. Much less one like Haley, who's so sweet and soft.

The way Leo looked at her in that church…

It wasn't just fairy-tale love. There was obsession, too. I think of his arms tensing around her that night in his office. *She's not leaving. Ever.* He would risk anything for Haley. Sneaking into a church would be the least he'd do for her.

Like it's the least Emerson would do for me.

My pulse races when I think about it like that. Leaving an orchid, even two orchids, even an expensive painting—those are games to Emerson. Like passing a note. It's different when he touches me.

When he has his mouth on me.

I shift on the seat, trying to get comfortable, trying to put these thoughts out of my mind. It's beyond me. I can't stop. It was the childish, safe Daphne who wanted a normal man. The artist in me has always been drawn to power. How could I not be? I've been walking on the shore of power all my life. I've never been allowed to swim.

Maybe that's what all these canvases filled with the ocean are about. Watching the water from the shore, never able to enter. Always apart.

"What about you?" I ask Eva.

"What about me?"

"Would you marry a Constantine?"

"No," she says, too quickly. "I would stay far away from Constantines."

"Why? Because of what happened?"

The driver makes a turn off the highway, and Eva looks at me, her expression careful. "What do you mean, because of what happened?"

"To Leo." I thought that was obvious. Nothing's ever been as personal as what happened to Leo.

"Oh." Eva glances out the window. "That, of

course. And because there's too much history between our families. Honestly, I don't trust them."

"Is that what you told Leo and Lucian?"

"I told Leo that, yes. But it was too late by then. He was already in love with her. Besides—Haley and Elaine. They're women."

"What, so they're nicer?"

"It's less about being nice and more about having power. Women don't run families like ours. The men do. I wouldn't trust one as far as I could throw him. No matter how charming he looks. Or how nice he seems. It's all a front."

I raise my eyebrow. "Do you have a particular one in mind?"

"Of course not." Eva shakes her head as if changing the subject. "I chose that champagne you like for the reception."

"That's why you're my favorite sister."

We talk about food and dancing and wedding guests until we join a row of cars in front of Leo's house. Gerard comes out to take our purses and usher us into the foyer.

The entire space has been redone for the wedding. No more dark wallpaper. Just by existing, Haley has made this place brighter—and there was already a ton of natural light before. We follow the decorations to the ballroom. I saw it this morning, but now, as the day wanes, it's even more beautiful.

Eva's taken the colors from the stained glass window—the rose and the white and the shadow—and pulled it into the room. Tiny glowing lights are everywhere.

It's a huge ballroom, but she's made it seem intimate.

"Wow," I breathe. "You're really good at this."

Eva kisses my cheek. "Go have some champagne. I'm going to make sure everything's okay."

It seems perfect so far. Leo and Haley are at one end of the room, talking to person after person. After a minute she covers her mouth with her hand and makes wide eyes at him. I know this look. Her lips are getting tired from smiling. He takes her hand in his and kisses her ring, then her cheek, and I think he'd kiss her more if she didn't laugh and put a hand on his jacket to stop him.

There's Eva, slipping easily through crowd, smiling, watching. The tall man from the ceremony and the engagement party—the Constantine-looking one, with the odd black eyes—is here with his beautiful wife, and with his dog. The dog sits so still at his side that most people don't notice it's here. Eva bends to pat its head, then continues on. I can see what she's saying as she goes. *Is there anything I can get for you? It's so good to see you. I'm so happy you could make it. Yes, he's very happy. She's a beautiful bride.* She circles all the way around to Leo and Haley. Leo turns his head to talk to Eva, and then both of them are looking in the same direction. He shakes his head. *Gerard will handle it.* Eva agrees.

"Nice ceremony," says my brother Carter. "Dragged a bit in the middle."

I turn around to give him a quick hug. "What, you don't like a full Mass for a wedding?"

His eyes glint with laughter. He stood up in the wedding, too. Carter's handsome like the rest of my brothers, but maybe less…vicious looking, if that makes any sense. Quieter. More serious. Though I've always suspected that he's just as hard beneath that surface. Harder, maybe.

He looks around to make sure no one can hear, then bends down so he can speak into my ear. "If anything could convince me to bind myself in that eternal hellscape, I'd elope."

This makes me laugh. A Morelli, just— eloping? Disappearing into the middle of nowhere and getting married without all of Bishop's Landing knowing about it? "You would not."

"How would anyone know? I'm away most of the time."

"You have a point." He does spend most of his time overseas doing some kind of work that's really prestigious. I don't know what it is, exactly. "Away doing what?"

He gives me a blank expression, which looks strange on his face, because he's always so damn knowledgeable all the time. "You know what I do."

"Research. On plants."

"Rhizomes, specifically. That's my area of expertise."

"Which are?"

"A subterranean plant stem that develops axillary buds and grows horizontally."

I laugh. "Are you telling me you study potatoes?"

A laughing glint enters his eyes. "Those are tubers. Rhizomes are turmeric, ginger. Bamboo."

"They keep you at Oxford to study bamboo?"

"Oh, God, they love when I study bamboo. The professors get sweaty when I talk about them. They're the thugs of the flora world. They spread faster than any other plant. Border grass. Chinese lanterns. You should see them when I talk about tansy. They come in their tweed pants."

I have to laugh at that. "I thought you were a spy or something."

"Yes," he says drily. "The government needs someone to study the terrorists known as weeds, destroying every flower bed outside their offices."

I stick out my tongue at him. "Are you staying the rest of the week?"

"I fly out tomorrow morning."

"But you just got in last night."

He shrugs. "My presence is required."

"For what? Are you meeting with the Queen or something?"

"Yes," he says with a wink. "She wants to know about the mysterious Daphne Morelli, the famous painter in New York City."

I snort. "Tell her I'm open for commissions."

Someone calls his name, and he pats my shoulder and leaves. I continue my quest for a server. Eva will want to make sure they're circulating appropriately.

Before I find the champagne, I find my mother. She's trying to make an exit from a conversation with two people I vaguely recognize from other Morelli parties. Her eyes land on me, and I see the moment she decides to use me as her excuse.

"My daughter," she says to them. "Come this

way," she murmurs when she's close enough. I fall into step and go with her to a standing table near the stained glass window. "How are you, sweetheart?"

"Good." It's an honest enough answer. I'm okay, and I also feel hyper-aware of everyone in here. There's no way Emerson gets into the reception. The church is one thing. Leo's house? No. But if he did, if he did. "How did you like the ceremony?"

"It was lovely." Her tone goes a little flat. "You and your sisters looked beautiful." She reaches out and fluffs at my hair. "And you seem so..." My mother studies my face, her eyes brighter than they normally are. Sharper. "You seem happy. Do you have news?"

I am practically shaking with anticipation for when Emerson texts me again. That's what news I have.

"Can I ask you a question?" I say instead.

"Of course."

"Did you love Dad when you got married?"

She lets out a short, surprised laugh. "What made you think of that?"

The way Leo looked today. His wedding was standing-room only, but he didn't seem to notice anyone else. Once Haley took her first step down the aisle, it was all over. I can't actually imagine my mother looking at my father that way. I can't imagine him looking at her that way.

"Just all the wedding stuff. Were you in love, do you think?"

Her eyes go slightly distant. Traveling through memories, maybe. Thinking back to their own wedding. I've seen the photos. My mother was beautiful on their wedding day, and my father was handsome. She's looking at him in a lot of the photos. He doesn't look back at her nearly as much.

"I was infatuated with him," she says finally. "Or maybe just the money and power he wielded. He's always had so much of it, and I thought…" My mother shakes her head. Her perfect red waves shake with her. "Don't make the same mistake."

A shiver sweeps down my back. "Don't marry rich?"

"Don't get obsessed," she says, her tone as light as mine. "Don't let infatuation cloud your judgement. But you wouldn't do that. Not my Daphne." An indulgent smile lifts the corners of her lips. "You've always been so good."

CHAPTER TWENTY-TWO

Emerson

IT'S BEEN TOO long since I've seen Daphne. Way too fucking long.

Going into that church and leaving her there was torture, and it hasn't ended.

Her absence is turning my own house against me. It's beginning to seem ominously large. It was never meant to be small, of course. I need room for the pieces I collect. But the outside world is seeping in through the windows. I try to force it back. My usual method is to surf more often. To let the size of the ocean overwhelm the size of the house.

It's not working.

Black waves beat at the shore outside. The last of the sunset bled out an hour ago. I've been out twice today. I have no desire to go again, but then I never want to in the first place.

Emerson: Tell me what you're thinking about, little painter.

If I focus, I can see my reflection in my bedroom window.

Some part of me knows that surfing won't be enough. That texting won't be enough. Maybe if Daphne were here—

No. I won't admit to feeling like this. To feeling anything like this.

What the fuck would I even say? *There's something I need to crush this into a manageable size.* This—what is this? She'd want to know. I'm not willing to use the word *panic* in conversation with her. With anyone. She'd never look at me the same way.

I need her to look at me the same way. Daphne was so scared when I spread her legs. I can still feel her hands shaking on my wrists. But she trusted me. She was afraid of me, and she trusted me. That trust would disappear from her eyes and never return.

Daphne: You

Emerson: What about me?

I pull up Sin's number on the screen and allow myself, for a single moment, to consider telling him.

My house feels like the fucking Grand Canyon.

I type it out and delete it. Sin would show up

here. He'd ask questions. He'd demand answers. I'm past that. My brothers and I are all past it.

The phone vibrates in my hand and my heart settles. Daphne. It'll be Daphne.

Alert: Front gate approach

Jesus. Is he ever going to learn to stay away? I type out a new text to Sin.

Emerson: I'm not interested in a visit.

Alert: Front gate entrance

So he's going to ignore me, then.

Sin: Good thing I'm out to dinner, then, asshole

Alert: Motion detected front door

A heavy knock echoes up the stairs. Something in the rhythm of it, in the sound, tugs at the oldest parts of my mind. I hold my breath. Stand perfectly still.

If it's not Sin, then who? Will? He wouldn't show up unannounced.

Not Daphne. Daphne would never try to beat down the door. Her hands are too small.

It happens again. Harder this time. And though I am within my rights not to open the front door ever again, for anyone, I move toward the noise. I want it to stop.

Alert: Motion detected front door

Yes, I know.

The handle resists me when I try to open it. Or it's my own body resisting. I don't know.

I pull harder. Force it.

My father stands on the porch.

He's dressed like a mid-level businessman. Pressed slacks. A red sweater under a tan overcoat. His hair has gone silver while he was in prison, but it retains a fair amount of its original dark. There's a vague humming in my ears. I've gone numb. My emotions are silent in their frames. Nowhere else to run.

"Hello, Emerson." He steps forward and puts his hand on my shoulder. "It's good to see you, son. You've done well for yourself. This is an expensive piece of property."

What a fucking liar. What a fake. I can hear how fake it is in his voice. "You should have said you were planning to visit."

"Didn't Sin tell you I was getting out?"

"He mentioned you were up for parole."

He waves this off and sidesteps me, crossing the threshold. "All done with that nasty business. I came to see you as soon as I could."

The last thing I want to do is close the door, locking him in with me, but it's a bitter night. "What do you want?"

"I don't want anything from you."

"Bullshit."

He bristles. "I've been in fucking prison, Emerson. I can't pay my own son a visit?"

"Is it money? I might have a twenty in my wallet."

"I don't need money, you little prick."

"Don't you? You're wearing the same clothes you wore to your last hearing."

"That's right." His flat, blue eyes take on a threatening glimmer. I never understood how my mother could ever look into those eyes. They're almost featureless, like a blank wall, like a blank soul. "They're the same goddamn clothes. None of my sons bothered to bring me anything new to wear after years of being caged like an animal."

A laugh bursts out of me. "I'm so sorry that happened to you. What must it have been like, trapped behind bars?"

He jabs a finger at me. "Don't talk to me about—"

"They let you out at least once a day, didn't they? You got to see the sun. You're such a pathetic fuck."

"And you're my most worthless son. What the fuck is this place, Emerson? A shrine to how much of a pussy you are?" He gestures at the art hanging in the entryway, sneering. "Look at you, still pretending the world is art so you don't have to admit you're terrified."

It occurs to me that the faint pounding in my head is an adrenaline rush. My father has never been inside my house before. I bought it after he went to prison, and I never thought he would come here. I was foolish, obviously. I should have taken Sin's announcement as a warning. I watch from outside my body as I shove my hand inside my pocket and come up with my wallet. Take a fifty-dollar bill between my fingers. Crumple it. Throw it on the floor at his feet.

"There. Now you're all taken care of."

My father looks down at the balled-up bill on the floor like it's roadkill. Like I spit at him. His eyes come up to mine, wide with rage. His nostrils flare.

And then he throws a punch at me.

For a split second it looks like the past come back to life. This was always how it started. An argument, followed by fists, followed by a door being slammed shut and locked from the outside. Back then I would have taken the hit. I would have let it happen, because fighting back only meant he'd try again. He was persistent that way.

But we're not in the past. We're very much in the present.

And I have the advantage of height and strength now.

He didn't make the most of his yard time in prison. He never tried to put on muscle. So I knock his fist away from my face and punch him back.

This is like punching a bull. It enrages him that I would dare, and he charges at me. What he lacks in strength he makes up for by being a psychotic piece of shit.

I have a sense of his shoulder near my chest somewhere, an elbow in my side, that fucking tan coat. Indignation rises. Who the fuck does he think he is, walking into my house like this? Where did he get the idea that this would end well for him?

It's not going to end well. I'm going to end him.

I back him up against the wall, an empty stretch with no painting, and punch him across the face. My knuckles connect with his cheekbone. His head snaps to the side. A younger version of me is wide-eyed with awe. My father always seemed unreachable back then. A goddamn giant. I'm surprised to find myself looking down at him. I'm surprised to find my fists buried in his sweater, and his wrists on mine. More than anything, I'm surprised to find realization dawning in his eyes. He's not going to win this fight.

"Fine," he spits. "Let me go."

I shake him instead. Rattle his head against the wall. "What if I want you to stay?"

"You don't want me to stay, you piece of—"

"What if I have the perfect place for you? We could play a game. We could see how long it would take for you to die." I pretend to calculate this. "You, alone in a room. How long would you make it? Two weeks? A month?"

"You're sick," he says, somehow managing to sound incredulous. As if he didn't make me this way himself. As if he didn't teach me how to be a bastard firsthand. He locked us in closets when we misbehaved. Or when we simply existed. Me. Sin. Even Will. He'd put us in closets without food or a fucking bathroom. It hurt to be in the closet, but it hurt even more to leave the closet—to see the bright sun, to breathe air that wasn't foul.

I punch him one more time, then drag him in close. "How long would I have to leave you in there until you went fucking crazy?"

The bastard twists, fighting to get free of my hands. I want to drag him to a shallow grave. I take him to the front door instead and throw him out into the night. He trips on one of his shoes but catches himself before he falls.

"Don't come back," I tell him, and then I slam the door. Lock it.

My phone buzzes over and over again.

Alert: Motion detected front door
Alert: Motion detected front door

I turn off the alerts and climb the stairs on autopilot. My own house yawns around me, every room looking like a cavern, every hallway looking like a funhouse mirror. My emotions are ripped off their canvases, torn from their frames. Out of control. What a shitshow. What an embarrassment.

Into the master bedroom, which takes up a quarter of the space on the second floor. Into the walk-in closet. No windows. A door that locks. My nerves scream. My head splits. Adrenaline feels like acid. I sit down hard in the farthest corner, my back to the wall.

No one else is in here.

No one.

No one.

My vision swims, and through the watery distortion I see the screen of my phone light up again.

Daphne: The way your tongue felt

No one's heartbeat can be this fast. It's not survivable. Jesus, I would do anything to have my head between Daphne's thighs right now.

Daphne: I want to see you

Not like this, she doesn't. Not like this.

But the suggestion is enough to pull me back from the brink.

Emerson: Then come see me.

I can practically see her hesitating. See her biting her lip.

I dial Sin's number next. He answers on the first ring. He wasn't lying about being out to dinner—silverware clinks in the background. Conversation rises and falls. The ambient sounds of somewhere expensive. "What the hell's going on with you?" he asks.

"Dad came to visit."

He curses under his breath. "And?"

"I threw him out."

"Alive?"

"Yes."

The conversation gets quieter. He must be going someplace else. "Are you okay?"

Fuck no. "This is a courtesy call to let you know that I gave him at least one black eye and he'll probably try to visit you next. I didn't give him the name of your hotel."

"I didn't think he would go to your place." Traffic now. Car tires on snow. He went outside. "I can come back. Are you still home? I can be there in forty-five—"

"No."

"Are you sure?"

"What the fuck would I want you here for?"

He's silent, and I feel a stab of guilt. Sin is one of two people on the planet who knows me at all, as much as I hate to admit it.

"Okay," he says finally. "I'll call Will. Let him know."

"You do that," I say, and then I hang up on him. There's nothing more to discuss.

Chapter Twenty-Three

Daphne

"I'M A PRISONER in my own life," I tell Eva.

She laughs at me over the phone. "Prison is an art supply store?"

"I mean, yeah, if you can't move about freely." I'm on the second floor of my favorite place to buy paint and canvas, and honestly, I don't need this long to pick out canvas. I'm here for the moment of peace. "They're everywhere."

"The security?"

"Yes. I didn't realize buying paint was such a high-stakes mission that it required two bodyguards. They're constantly breathing down my neck."

"Literally? Like right now?"

I sigh. "Not literally. They're downstairs. If you tell Leo I left them on a separate floor—"

"I would never betray you like that. You know, you have to tell him if you don't like the guys. He'll get—"

"He'll get new ones," I finish for her. "But I

don't want guards, Eva. I want to buy paint."

"They're not going to stop you from buying paint," she soothes. "You just moved back into your place. The guards are only temporary."

I snort. "They are not temporary. There are even more of them in the apartment across the street."

"It's because—"

"Because I had a stalker." I make air quotes with my free hand even though Eva can't see me. "Now I shall forever pay the price."

"He hasn't come back into your apartment, has he?"

"Not that I know of."

"Daphne! That's not funny. Has he been there?"

"No," I promise. I turn a corner onto another row of canvases.

That's when I feel someone watching.

The hair on the back of my neck rises before I can fully register the sensation, but that's what it is—someone is watching. Goose bumps flare between my shoulder blades. I whip my head around, looking over the aisles.

Nothing is out of place. An old lady with shaky hands compares two canvases at the other end of the shop. A couple has a hushed debate over which size to buy. A store employee carries a box out from a storage area in the back.

"Daphne?"

"Yeah?"

"Can you still hear me?"

"I can." My heart pounds.

"Did something happen?"

"I thought someone was looking at me. It's probably the security assholes creeping up from downstairs to make sure I'm safe from this old lady and all this canvas." I turn back around and hunch over, dropping my voice. "I can't live like this forever. I can't have people constantly watching me because Leo's paranoid."

"I'll talk to him." Eva's decisive. A problem-solver. "See if you can go back to the way things were. As long as nothing shady has happened, it should be—"

"No, don't do that. It's fine." I don't want Leo to think I'm being an ungrateful brat. I also don't want him to think I'm not capable of speaking up for myself. "Just venting."

"You want to come over when you're done at the store?"

I'm about to say no when all the hairs on the back of my neck stand up. "What about lunch? I know it's kind of late, but…"

"Late lunch is perfect." She names a restaurant not far from the art supply store, and I agree. I leave the canvases and buy some paints. My two shadows are posted at the exit in their suits. One of them opens the door for me and I push past while the other hurries out ahead of me. Two bodyguards and a separate driver, all to buy a little paint.

"Did you come up to the second floor to check on me?" I ask the one who's closing the car door.

He blinks. "No, ma'am. Was someone bothering you?"

"No," I say quickly. "No one bothered me."

But someone watched me. I felt it. Twice.

Eva and I have lunch together at a corner table that the security guards choose for us. They don't like for me to sit by the window.

"See?" I whisper to her as we sit down. "This is way over the top. Is something happening I don't know about?"

"If something's happening, I don't know about it either," she reassures me.

"You would tell me?"

"Yes." My suspicion must show in my eyes. "I'm serious, Daph. I would tell you if I'd heard anything. Are you okay?"

I feel it again—that unmistakable sensation of being watched. If I turn to look, to search, Eva's going to know.

She narrows her eyes. Clearly I haven't been as stealthy as I thought. "Would you tell me if something was happening?"

"Of course I would."

"You know…" Eva drums her fingers on the white linen tablecloth, her expression thoughtful. She looks just like Leo, except more beautiful. More regal. "You don't have to tell me anything, Daph. It's up to you what you share, or don't share. I'm only asking because I care about you and I want you to be happy."

"Leo says the same thing. Did you guys coordinate your message?"

"Nope, no message coordination going on." Eva laughs. "Surprisingly, we didn't spend a lot of time chatting while he and Haley were on their honeymoon."

"I wonder if bodyguards followed them around the entire time," I grumble, softening it with a smile.

"They did."

"Oh, stop."

Eva widens her eyes. "I'm serious. He even had people on a ship circling the private island."

I laugh out loud. "A ship? Those people are never going to let him take a vacation there again."

"They don't own the island anymore. He bought it."

"Wow." I lean back in my seat. "So what you're saying is, stop complaining about the two bodyguards."

"I know it's not much consolation, but Leo's not doing this because he's paranoid. That's when you think people are out to get you and you don't have any proof. People *are* out to get him."

It's annoyingly reasonable. "Yeah, but I'm nobody."

"You are Daphne Morelli," Eva says, lifting her wine glass in my direction. "You might want to be no one, but you're not. You won the genetic lottery. You're one of us."

"And that means bodyguards."

"It means paying attention." Eva sips her wine. "It means knowing who's paying attention to you."

Well, I already know that. It's Emerson. We're inside, well away from the door, but I feel another whisper of cold on the nape of my neck. If he's in here right now, watching me eat lunch with Eva...

"Who's paying attention to you?" I ask Eva.

"Nobody at all, which is how I like it."

"Sure they're not. You want me to believe that nobody saw you at the Christmas gala or at Leo's wedding? Nobody tried to ask you on a date?"

"No one tried to ask me on a date." I know, I just know, that she's being specific in this way because someone talked to her but they didn't ask her to dinner. Eva flushes slightly.

"Who was it?"

"There was no date," she insists, but her resolve doesn't last. "I ran into Finn Hughes at the gala. He helped me with the mince pies."

The mince pies were ruined at Christmas. Actually they were fine, but our mother didn't think they were up to par. I put a hand to my chest.

"I'm offended. I offered to help you, and you invited Finn Hughes down to the kitchen instead?"

"Please. He wandered in."

"So you—" I bat my eyes at her, exaggerated enough to make her laugh. "*Oh, Finn, please, I couldn't possibly fix these mince pies by myself.*"

"Yes, Daphne. It was exactly like that."

I remember her talking about how she'd never marry a Constantine. Finn Hughes doesn't share the last name, but he's in their family tree. Is that who she was thinking about? *I wouldn't trust one as far as I could throw him. No matter how charming he looks. Or how nice he seems. It's all a front.*

We move on from Christmas to Leo's wedding and then to general Bishop's Landing gossip. Eva hears a lot, though she lives in the city. I'm lulled by her stories and the chance to tell her about my paintings and I almost, *almost*, forget that every move I make is being watched.

Until it happens again.

This time I turn my head to the side and try to find the watcher. No one meets my eyes. No one looks in my direction. It's a restaurant full of people eating a lunch that's basically a dinner at this point. No hint of Emerson's blue-green eyes. No hint of his hair, or the way he stands. Nothing, nothing, nothing.

"What is it?" Eva peers around me, trying to see what I'm looking for. "Somebody here?"

"No," I tell her. "I thought I heard my name."

I thought I felt eyes on me. I *know* I felt eyes on me. Unless I'm losing my sense of reality. That happens to artists sometimes. They get lost in a piece, or in a project, and the real world fades away.

That's not what's happening to me. My concentration on my work lasts an hour at most, and then I'm back to thinking of Emerson.

The bodyguards accompany me home from lunch in a black SUV. I'm not supposed to take Ubers anymore—Leo doesn't think it's safe. And yet...the SUV didn't stop someone from watching me in the art supply store, or the restaurant.

By the time I close the apartment door behind me, it's a pressure on my skin. My heart races. Someone is watching. I know they are, and I think I know who it is. I perch in the window seat in my bedroom and look down on the street below.

I'm tired of waiting.

The thought trickles in, tiny drops of realization that slowly fill my gut.

I'm tired of waiting for him to get closer and closer until he catches me. That night at the gallery. The painting in my apartment. The flowers. Emerson talks to me over text with the kind of infinite patience that tells me he has a plan. He's in no rush because he's made a decision about me. He wants me, and he's going to keep doing this, and I am tired of playing games.

I want to be the one to choose. No more

waiting for him to reveal himself. He's already shown me what he's capable of. The lock on the door of this place won't keep him out.

I don't want it to keep him out.

I want to go to him.

Daphne: Are you in the city?

His reply takes almost no time.

Emerson: Yes.
Daphne: Can you come get me?
Emerson: Are you hurt?

No. No, I am not hurt. I want out of this pressure around my ears, around my head. I want out of this little apartment with the security off this street. I want a few minutes where nobody is watching me.

Except Emerson.

Daphne: I want to go with you. I'm not hurt. Can you come?

I put my coat back on and transfer my essentials to the pockets. My purse feels like too much of a burden right now. All I need is my slim wallet and my phone. I'll be back before long, and when I come back, I'll be able to breathe.

Emerson: Ten minutes.

The traffic gets heavier over the next ten minutes. My security guards pull the SUV into an alley down the street. They change shifts. New guards take their posts. Afternoons are so short in January. The days are short. It's basically dark when I turn on a soft lamp in my living room and text the people on the night shift.

Daphne: I'm in for the night!!

It makes me feel lightheaded to lie. It makes my heart pound with guilt. But they just text back a thumbs-up emoji. I brush my teeth and go back to watching the traffic.

Emerson: Are you ready, little painter?

Daphne: Yes, but I don't see you

Emerson: Go out through the alley. Opposite way. Turn left and walk two blocks.

Daphne: Okay

I get up and go before I can change my mind. The last thing I grab is my keys, to lock the door. Down the stairs. A moving shadow scares the shit out of me at the bottom and I freeze.

Robert. In the gallery. He hasn't locked up yet. In a few minutes, he'll be coming through to the outside.

Now or never. If I go back upstairs, I'll lose my nerve. So I don't. I tiptoe down the last two steps, lean my head out to make sure he's gone back into the main gallery, and slip out the alley door.

It's like being hit with a wall of snow. Every sense is alive. I smell bitter wind and concrete, feel the breeze playing with my hair. Please, let them not be watching the alley right now. Please let them not be watching. I walk close to the wall, trying to hide in the shadows, and reach the other end of the alley.

Turn left.

Two blocks.

I keep expecting footsteps to run after me. For my name to echo off the buildings. Half a block down. A full block. I look both ways and cross the street. I don't see him—I don't see Emerson. Dread and shame make my throat tight. Would he trick me like this? Lure me? Eva said that being a Morelli is about paying attention, and what did I do? I snuck away from my security to meet a dangerous man.

I'm a third of the way down the second block and about to turn back when a dark gray SUV glides to the curve. The back door opens.

Emerson steps onto the sidewalk and holds out his hand to me. I break into a run, like there's someone chasing me, and let him help me into the car. It's warm inside. It smells new and like him. He wastes no time sitting down and pulling the door closed.

His driver pulls back into traffic. I'm breathing hard, my eyes glued on the sidewalk. Emerson's watching, too. We pass by the alley that leads to my place. It's blessedly empty. As soon as he sees it is, he turns back to me with those stunning eyes, with that face.

"I made it," I tell him. I'm gripping my collar for dear life. This is the most reckless thing I've ever done. The worst thing I've ever done. It's bad. And it feels good.

"You're very brave." Pride glimmers in his eyes. "I promise it'll be worth it."

CHAPTER TWENTY-FOUR

Emerson

I'T'S SHADOWED IN the back of the SUV as we coast over the highway. Distant city lights play over her face, her little nose, her delicate chin. Daphne's dark eyes catch every bit of that glow. They glimmer. She's so proud of herself. She's such a brave little painter. I meant what I said. I meant every word.

I keep myself on the opposite side of the SUV, in the darker shadows. The sweet, cold-air smell of her fills every breath I take. It's shoving sensation into my face, into my skin. I have to push it away again and again. Turn it into art. In a frame. Trapped. Still. So what if I'm turning this moment into an approximation of canvas? I'm not afraid of Daphne, or kissing her, or fucking her. I'm staying in control.

I want to lunge on her, but I won't. I've had years of practice with waiting.

Never mind the bristling feeling I've been living inside since my front door closed behind that bastard.

I don't want to scare her.

Even if it is inevitable.

Because, of course, I don't want a few stolen moments at a charity gala. A man doesn't steal precious items, he acquires them. And then he keeps them very, very safe. He binds them to him by virtue of his protection and his ownership. With art, this happens with money. With contracts and certificates and records of provenance.

It will be different with Daphne. Protection and ownership, yes. But not with money. I am already aware of her provenance. I know where she came from. And I know where she'll be, starting tonight. The process of binding—of breaking, perhaps—that will take longer.

I can be patient.

Despite the rush of blood in my head, in my veins, in my cock. Despite the pull to her. Like an undertow. Like a riptide. It's almost painful to resist it, but I do. I will. For a little while longer. I flatten it out. Turn it to face the wall.

"Tell me something."

"What?"

"How is it that I was the first man to lick your cunt?"

Daphne gasps, but she recovers quickly. She'd let her hand down from her collar but it flies back up to the soft sweater underneath her jacket. "I wasn't lying about that."

"I didn't think you were."

She becomes a silhouette edged in moonlight as we turn off the highway and toward the water. "I didn't date anyone. Not like that. I let a couple of guys take me out, but I never went home with anyone. I never wanted things to get that far. Not in high school, and not in college."

I like this about her, in a possessive, animal way. I like that no other man has ever touched her, or seen her sweet pussy. But concern prickles. "Because you're not interested in sex?"

I doubt that very much. The way she came in my mouth was desperate and lovely. She wanted it.

"Because it seemed…" Daphne considers this carefully. "It seemed dangerous to get my heart broken. My friends would date. They'd fall in love and break up, and they were so devastated by all of it."

"But not you."

"My brother is very protective."

Not her parents. My view of her family shifts again. In my experience with families like the

Morellis, it's usually the parents with an iron grip on the daughters. Daughters, after all, can be pressured into advantageous marriages. Families like Daphne's aren't consolidating property anymore, like in feudal England. They're consolidating generational wealth.

"The brother you were staying with?"

"Yes. Leo." Daphne folds her hands in her lap. "Once, when I was eleven, one of the boys from my class followed me to my locker. He said—" She makes a huffing sound, as if she still can't quite believe it. "He said that all the Morellis were thieves and murderers, and everyone would be happier if I hurried up and went to hell."

"What the fuck?"

"I'm not saying my family is perfect." She watches me very carefully now, waiting to see how I'll react. "But it was…a lot. And then he said that everyone hated my art. He said I'd only won the art contest that year because everyone was afraid of my father."

"Fuck him."

"I didn't win because of him. My piece was good." The note of confidence in her voice is the sexiest thing for how fleeting it is. "Anyway, I was too hurt to brush it off. Leo saw my face when I got home, and of course I told him everything.

The next day he waited outside the school for that kid to come out, and he scared the shit out of him." A stifled laugh. "That boy never looked at me again. I don't know exactly what Leo said, but everyone was super nice to me after that. So…" Daphne sighs. "If somebody broke my heart—like, really broke it—I don't even know what he'd do."

Interesting. She's not much for one-night stands, then. And the brother—I can understand protectiveness. I'd like to go back in time and break the bones of whoever would speak to Daphne that way. But I want more for her than that.

I want more *from* her.

She bites at her lip, excitement flickering into her eyes. "Are we going to the beach?"

My god. Daphne thinks we're going on a little adventure. That she's having a moment of rebellion that will be over by sunrise.

She doesn't know I'm not going to give her back. I'm not going to let her go.

"Yes," I say, because it's the simple truth. "We're going to the beach."

Our first stop is, indeed, my beach. I take her to the lip of the water and let her breathe in the night air. Daphne stands close to me, shivering in her coat, her hands shoved into her pockets. Waves roll to shore, rippling in the moonlight. She studies each crest, each fall.

"My hands are shaking too much to paint," she says softly. "It's so cold."

"You'll be warm inside." I put my hand on the small of her back and guide her across the sand to another staircase carved out of the retaining wall. This one leads to my house.

We crest the wall, and Daphne sucks in a surprised breath. From this vantage point the house is all light pouring from massive windows. All the curtains have been pushed back. I wanted it to look welcoming and safe. I can tell from the shine in her eyes that it does. I won't be leading her into a dark, obscured space.

I take her in through a side door leading to an oversized entryway. My wetsuit hangs here, and three surfboards. There's plenty of room left over for a changing bench. Daphne shivers happily in the heat. "That's nice."

"You won't need this." I slip her coat off her shoulders and feel her little tenses as my fingers make contact with her sweater. So close to her skin.

Daphne kicks her boots off and takes a tentative step toward the hall. She'll find my den there, and if she goes further, my office. My dining room. The kitchen.

"Go," I tell her. "Look around. I'm just going to hang up my coat."

She pads away, excitement in her eyes. Daphne will be curious, and I want to give her a minute to acclimate herself without being watched. I take off my gloves. My coat. Hang them up.

I want to give myself a moment, too. Having her inside the threshold is a relief. Daphne is the living embodiment of pure emotion, and emotion like that—dark, alive, entrancing—is dangerous. Deadly. It's better for both of us if she becomes a gallery piece.

Next, I take her phone out of her coat pocket.

My little painter doesn't have a security code. That makes it significantly easier to wipe the location data from the last two hours. Her iPhone hasn't uploaded to the cloud yet—she hasn't been connected to wifi. I disable the location services. That takes a password, which Daphne stores in her Notes app. It takes less than a minute. When I'm finished, I put it back into her coat pocket. It's unlikely she'll come looking for it tonight, but if she does, it will be here.

I line up my shoes next to hers. The sight of them side by side.

Daphne is in the den, looking up at the wall.

At her own painting.

I want to touch her so badly. I want to put my hand around her throat and tug her back against me.

I do not.

"How did you get this?"

I hang back a little. It's getting more difficult to keep my distance. "I bought it."

"It wasn't for sale." The first hint of suspicion crosses her gorgeous dark eyes. "I donated it to the department."

"They were willing to make a deal."

She keeps looking.

"Daphne." Her eyes snap to mine, and not for the first time, I am bowled over by how beautiful she is. How delicate. How innocent. "I didn't bring you here to visit my den."

Curiosity burns to life with another heat behind it. "What, then?" Daphne tries to sound casual, but she doesn't.

I gesture to the door. There's a tearing sensation in my chest. I need to touch her, and I need to push her away. I need to fuck her but I need to put her in a frame and bolt her to the wall before I lose myself completely.

Not now.

Not yet.

For the moment, I allow myself to feel anticipation.

We reach the landing at the top of the stairs
and she hesitates again. Half of the upper floor is
the master suite, the layout mirrored on the other
side. Between the two suites is the room I need
Daphne to see.

"Through here."

I take her into my bedroom. Daphne's eyes
light up at the windows. I reach behind her for
the switch that turns down the lamps. The ocean
springs into view under the moon. She can't
decide where to look. My bed? The hallway
leading to my closet and bathroom? An enormous
shaft of light falls from the open double doors in
the left-hand wall.

Daphne's drawn to it. I knew she would be.

It takes only the gentlest touch to send her
into motion toward that light. It falls over her face
first, then her body. Her perfect lips part. And
then she steps into what I've made for her.

"Emerson," she breathes.

In its former life, this was a living room of
sorts. An oversized den with a wall of windows.

Now it's an art studio. New hardwood floors.
White walls. Windows upon windows. And

shelves full of anything she could dream of. Canvases. Paints. Brushes.

A few more steps into the room.

A single canvas waits on an easel near the windows. A small table rests nearby for paints and brushes. A stool, too.

"This is huge." Daphne's astonished. "This is so lovely." She cannot help herself. She goes into this space I made for her and paces around it. Circles the canvas. She goes to the shelves on the other side of the wall and skims her fingers over the paints, the brushes.

"There are more supplies in the drawers," I tell her.

Daphne bends and opens one, then another, her face lighting up again and again. They are all arranged in neat rows. They are all pristine, untouched. Waiting for her. The studio can never surpass her loveliness. This moment is so poignant that I push the throb in my heart away gently.

My little painter gets to the last shelf and straightens up. "It's like…"

She doesn't finish the sentence. It fades from her lips at the same time her smile does. Daphne's eyes go back to the easel. To the shelves on the opposite wall.

"It's bright in here," she mentions, a quaver in

her voice.

I'm close enough to reach the panel of switches on the wall. Most of the lights fall, but one remains. It shines down directly on the easel.

This doesn't make things better for Daphne. Her eyes get wider, and she backs up a step. It looks involuntary. She hooks a hand into her collar.

It's right there, on her face. In those luminous dark eyes.

Worry. Verging on fear.

"We're not together," she says. "But you made this for me?"

"Yes."

"It's like a pedestal. Where you'd put a sculpture in a house. Where you—where you could look at me."

Enough waiting. I cross the room to her and take her face in my hands, tilting it up so she meets my eyes. "When I look at you, what does it feel like?"

Daphne's lips press together, then part again. Jesus Christ. "It's intense. And I like it."

"It makes you wet. Are you wet right now?"

"Yes," she whispers.

"Are you afraid?"

"Why am I here, Emerson?"

AMELIA WILDE

I run a soothing hand over her hair and her shoulders relax. "You wanted to see me. You asked me to come get you, and I did."

"No." She straightens her spine. "Why am I here, in this room?"

"You already know that, little painter."

Daphne looks into my eyes. I see the desperate search there. I want her to turn her face away, to stop looking, but I know this is a necessary step. She will need to see that I want her. She will need to remember, all on her own, the conversation we've already had.

"You want to watch me paint the ocean," she murmurs. "You brought me here to paint?"

"While I watch."

I deliver this low and soft, because this is a crucial moment. Daphne's eyes are locked on mine. It's very nearly unbearable. I'm turning it into art second by second. Frame by frame. It feels fucking filthy to do it. Resentment flashes through me. Hurt. It's been chipping away at my resolve. What that bastard said cut into me, though I'll never admit it. It's shaken something at the foundation of me. The world keeps breaking through, breaking in.

No. None of that now. Only Daphne. Focus on her eyes. On her face. The shadows playing there, the light. Her expanded pupils. Trust me, little painter. Don't look too close.

"I think—" So tentative. "I think I would like that."

As if she's asking me. As if she wants my permission for her to like it. Jesus fuck. By the time I'm done with her, she'll be formed to me. Commissioned for me.

"You don't think, little painter. You know."

"I know you want more. You told me you want more."

"I'm going to take more."

At *take*, her lashes flutter closed for a split second, her chin tilts up, and her balance shifts ever so slightly toward me.

"I want that," she says. "I want you to take more from me."

I lean down and kiss her. Daphne's tongue meets mine. She lets me in. It feels like falling. I have to arrest the drop. Just a little longer now. For her. So she won't try to escape.

When I pull back, her hands come up and twist into my shirt. I let her hold on for a beat. Brush my thumb over her cheekbone.

"Be brave for me." Daphne nods. *Humming-bird*, I think. Quick. Flighty. Delicate. "Go over to your canvas and take off all your clothes."

CHAPTER TWENTY-FIVE

Daphne

THE ONLY EASY thing is the walk to the easel. I've walked up to a canvas a million times in my life. Except this one has a spotlight. The spotlight reflects in Emerson's huge windows. I won't be able to see the ocean like this. I'll have to paint it by memory.

I'll have to paint it with my pulse beating in my ears and all of my skin flushed with heat.

I've imagined this moment every day since Emerson first asked me to come with him. I never imagined I'd be brave enough to do this. Or reckless enough to do this. I never imagined I would feel this much guilt.

Or desire.

Except when I get to the canvas, and find myself under that light, I can't do it.

Emerson is opening drawers, moving around the room, gathering things. And I'm frozen. I try to get my bearings. There's a little table near the easel, narrow and tall, and a stool. I haven't moved at all when he slides a palette onto the table. Lays out three brushes.

"Choose," he says.

I force myself to look at him. He has a portable case of paints open in his hands, and it's momentarily distracting enough to ground me. White. Black. Different blues. I pull them out and try not to think. Emerson takes the case away while I put paint onto the palette. It's made for oil paints. Wooden and solid and traditional.

This is the least traditional painting I've ever done.

I set it back down.

Emerson moves behind me and skims his hand over my elbow. He did this that night in the gallery, too. I remember it. It calms me. I don't know how he knows to do this. To move his hand slowly up my arm to the side of my neck.

"Are you embarrassed?"

I've never been naked in front of a man before, and now I'm in an actual spotlight, reflected in the window. "Yes."

His hand moves down. Slides under my sweater. Works into the fabric of my leggings. I stop breathing. His fingers move gently between my legs.

"The little painter likes a bit of shame," he

comments. Emerson pulls his hand away. "But you're testing my patience."

Warning edges his tone, and my heart pounds. He's eaten me before. I can be brave for him. I can do this.

Emerson steps back as I pull my sweater over my head, and then my tank top. At first I think it's to give me space.

Then I see him in the reflection.

He's a shadow at the edge of the light but his eyes gleam. He's looking at me the way he looked at my paintings in the gallery.

I should be indignant, that he's seeing me as an object right now.

I'm not indignant.

I'm simultaneously ashamed and hot for it.

Leggings next. The socks I wore underneath.

Emerson moves back in as I'm wriggling out of my panties, out of breath, my cheeks burning. When I straighten up he puts his hand on my elbow again. I already know this touch. I know how he'll run it up my arm, to my shoulder, to the side of my neck—

He makes a collar of his hand, and I can't breathe. I can't move. His grip is more command-ing than it was in the gallery, and I'm wearing far less clothing. With his other hand, he makes soothing strokes down my arm.

"One more," he says.

I lift shaking hands to take off my bra and drop it to the floor. He's closer now. His expensive clothes brush against my back. He's hard underneath those clothes. Every part of him is hard—abs, chest, cock.

"Such a good little painter," he murmurs into my ear. "Now pick up your paints."

I have to bend to do it. The motion pushes my ass against him. He doesn't give at all. He wants to do this. I'm on fire with shame, and with this heat between my legs, and with his hand on my throat. I have a brush in my hand, though I don't remember choosing one. I have the paint.

"Deep water," Emerson says. "Paint how it feels right now." He moves me around to the front of the stool by the throat and tugs me onto it. I have to step back and up, but I make it. And then I'm painfully aware of how naked I am.

Protests rise to my tongue and drown in his touch. I normally start with a sketch. But his hand across my airway, his other hand playing at my hip, the hard stool under soft flesh, oh my god— it's all so much that I don't know how to sketch.

The moment hangs.

And I understand.

He's going to be still—he won't touch me, won't take this further until I paint.

Blue goes onto the brush.

The moment I touch it to the canvas, his hands move. One stays firm on my throat while the other presses flat on my belly and rises to circle my nipples with a fingertip. I paint the suggestion of a wave, way up near the top of the canvas. Add black near the bottom. I hardly have any control over my brushwork. I don't know how I'm supposed to, when Emerson's touching me. Goose bumps chase after every trace of my skin. It's like I'm being outlined. It's like he's finding my edges.

I want him to find another place.

But I don't have the words to beg him for it. I'm concentrating too hard on painting. I'm trying to ignore the fact of my body's responses. Not because it doesn't feel good, but because it feels so good that I'm losing my composure. I'm in the middle of filling in a swath of roiling blue when I discover myself rocking on the edge of the stool, my thighs spread for him without Emerson having to say a word.

He notices at the same time I do—or maybe he's waited for me to notice first.

Slowly, tortuously, he runs his hand down to

my thigh. All the way to my knee. He skims his fingers back up. I open for him even more, making furious swipes with the brush.

He avoids the wet, aching place I want him to touch and a frustrated noise escapes me.

Emerson laughs. He smells so good, like an icy wind with a core of warmth, a hint of something spicy and male. His laugh is delighted.

It's almost cruel.

He rolls one of my nipples between his thumb and forefinger. Pleasure feels like the roots of a plant, driving deep into the ground in thin tendrils. It reaches down the length of my body. I want him to touch me. I want him to make me come. And he is touching me, but not where I need.

Layers of paint go onto the canvas. The water is so choppy it looks like it's going to explode into my face. Arousal drips down the inside of my thigh. Oh, Jesus. On instinct I try to close my legs, to hide it from him, but Emerson's hand blocks me. He yanks my thighs back open and squeezes at my throat. A bolt of real fear flashes through me. He must feel it, because he wraps his other arm around me and holds me still.

"Shh," he says into my ear. "Just paint."

He will not touch my clit.

He won't do it.

Frustration heats and boils over. Emerson's big, strong hand is everywhere but where I need it to be, and look at me, look at me. I'm a naked woman perched on a painting stool with her legs spread wide, practically begging, and he is giving me nothing.

I begged him to wait before. Maybe this is why he's doing this. I'm electric with nervousness and shame and a twisting desire. How long do I last? Another five minutes? Ten?

"Please," I hear myself say. "I need to come. I need you to touch me."

"Not yet, little painter."

"What are you waiting for? This is mean. This is so mean."

"I never promised to be nice," I think he says. I can't quite hear. My heartbeat is too loud. The emptiness in my pussy is too much. Every breath hurts. Keeping my thighs open like this hurts. The fact that he won't help me—it hurts.

One tear slips down my cheek, and then a second. I keep the brush on the canvas. Emerson makes a sound behind me. He approves of this. He wants this. He wanted me to cry.

"You're doing this on purpose," I gasp.

"Yes," he agrees. "Does it feel good to cry?"

"No." It's a lie. It does feel good to release some of this pressure. "This isn't what I need."

He leans close to speak into my ear. "This isn't about what you need. I wanted to see what this looks like on your face, and your body."

"This?"

"Emotion. Tears." Another low laugh. "Desperation."

A chill runs down my spine. "You built me an art studio," I argue back, more tears falling, faster now. A sob hitches at my chest. I'm so frustrated. "Give me what I need."

Emerson groans. "Oh, little painter. The sight of you coming apart."

I'm not coming apart, I mean to say, but then he pushes two fingers inside me and the paintbrush falls to the floor.

This is what I needed, and it's also much more than I thought it would be. They feel thick inside me. Almost thicker than I can take. But Emerson fucks me with them like he's confident in my abilities.

He pulls them out again, sweeps a paintbrush from the table, and puts it back in my hand.

Emerson pushes his fingers in deep and waits.

My hand shakes as I move the bristles back toward the canvas. I have never been touched this way before. Holy Christ.

"That's it," he coaxes. "Let me see you, and I'll give you what you want. Fuck, you're wet for this."

More tears drip down to my thighs, each one a hot pinprick.

"This is humiliating," I whisper. "This is awful."

"I could take my fingers away. Would that feel better?"

He forces me to admit it. Out loud. "No."

The brush meets the canvas. Emerson's fingers move again. Slow, deep strokes.

I add more blue, more white. I am painting dark swirls of power. I am painting secrets, and frustration, and want. I am painting the shame of being finger-fucked while he orders me to paint and the unbelievable sexiness of it. The tips of his fingers are near to reaching the place inside that he's going to have to break. I've lost all sense of the sea. I don't know how far the surface is. Emerson's not just holding my throat anymore. I've leaned into it, wanting more pressure or unable to hold myself up or both. My hips roll forward onto his fingers. The brush stays on the canvas.

"Is this what you wanted?" I manage to say,

the words broken up by my panting. "When you said you wanted more?"

"I wanted you naked. I wanted you crying."

"Why?"

In and out. In and out.

"Because," he says. "It's so beautiful."

It's so beautiful.

Not *you.*

He puts his thumb on my clit.

All the sensation, all the pleasure, crashes into that single bundle of nerves and explodes. I come hard on his fingers and lose my balance completely. He holds me up, holds me back from the floor, but I drop the paintbrush again and one of my hands goes into fresh paint.

"Fuck," he says, and if I didn't know better, I'd think he was desperate, too. Some inner part of me collapses. My shame overheats into something else. Maybe I am naked. Maybe I am crying. But he's here with me. "Up, little painter. Now."

My legs aren't steady. I let him guide me behind the stool and bend me over it. Oh, no—I'm going to leave a handprint the color of my shame. I'm so lightheaded.

"I can't paint anymore," I tell him on a shuddering breath. I never once imagined that I would lose my virginity like this.

Emerson edges my legs apart with his foot against the inside of mine. I'm expecting a zipper but instead I hear the soft meeting of fabric against wood.

And then.

His tongue.

On my pussy.

I start to cry in earnest now from sheer relief. This angle is different and new and embarrassing. He has to hold me open to do it. I grip the edge of the stool like it can save me. His tongue is everywhere. Pushing in. Tasting. He licks me so furiously that through the haze in my mind I think it must be for a purpose. Another orgasm pulls me under, thrashes me around, and tosses me out again. The sounds I make are unrecognizable. So much. It's so much.

Emerson stands up behind me, and now I do hear his zipper. Now I do hear the sharp breath he takes. It makes me feel unbearably close to him. I'm not the only one in this. I'm not the only one who needs this.

"I'm going to fuck you now. Can you be brave?"

"Yes." My thighs tense with fear. I have honestly no idea how much this will hurt. I only know that I want it. "Please."

Emerson strokes a hand down my back, down to my hip, and adds a little pressure. *Stay still*, that pressure says. He nudges my thighs a little farther apart with his free hand. Then, for a moment, both his hands are on my lower back. One last touch.

And then the head of him presses against my opening. I'm wet from his mouth, and wet from my own orgasms, but it still feels huge. Bigger than his fingers by far. There's an automatic urge to get away, but Emerson holds me in place. His hands go to my hips. He's working his way in. The wide head of him.

He's huge.

My head goes up. "Yes. That's it." He moves my hips for me, rocking them back against him in tiny motions that would seem ridiculous if they weren't working. If they weren't opening me up for him. Emerson groans. "You're so tight," he says. "You're squeezing my cock so tight."

I want more of that. I want more of the emotion in his voice. And so I try harder to take him.

It's not easy.

I have to stretch. To work at it. I'm covered in a sheen of sweat. Emerson slips one hand around to my clit and rubs at it in slow circles. I can feel myself melting around him.

I can feel him meeting that barrier inside.

There's pressure there. It doesn't belong. He wants past it. I want him to be past it.

"Take a deep breath." His voice is the most gorgeous thing I've ever heard. I want it all over me. "Open your thighs. It's all right."

They'd started to slide shut, but I open them wide again, try to angle myself for him. It feels better this way. But the pressure is still there.

"I have to hurt your cunt so I can fuck you." Emerson's voice is level, but there's tension at the edges.

I'm shivering. I feel practically delirious. "You want to hurt me other ways," I hear myself say. "You like for me to cry."

"I do want to hurt you other ways," he admits. "It would make you so wet, little painter. It would make your cunt clench so hard. Oh, fuck. Just like that. It would make your pussy tighten just like that."

I let out an embarrassed moan. He said he wanted to hurt me, and I liked it. I don't know who I am anymore.

I would let him do it. I want to give him this. I want Emerson to take it. The darkness I have inside of me. The shame. The hurt. I want him to fuck it out of me. I want him to hurt me in whatever way he's talking about.

Here, with him, I'm allowed to want that.

Emerson lets out another groan. Thinking of him that way—thinking of him with control over my body that way—it almost makes me come again. Oh, Jesus, I'm desperate to be past this place. I'm desperate to have all of him inside of me. I rock back against him, struggling, pushing.

"So brave," he says. "So good. You can cry, little painter. Let it out. Cry for me. Let me see everything."

One powerful thrust of his hips, and he tears into me. He warned me but I'm still shocked. The scream gets free before I can stop it.

Emerson curses, again and again, while I sob. He's fucking me through this pain. Hard, cruel strokes.

"Take it. You can take it. It'll feel better soon." His fingers find my clit again. I don't believe him. He's broken me irreparably. I'm about to tell him when the stinging pain begins to fade.

I try to get up from the stool. He can fuck me on the floor. Or in his bed. "I want to see your face. Please. Emerson, please."

His hand comes down on the back of my neck and turns my head forward.

"Just for a minute," I plead. I want his arms around me for a minute. I want to see the blue-green perfection of his eyes. I want to kiss him. I want to feel how close we are. I want to feel even closer.

"Don't turn your head."

"I want to. Please. I want—"

He reaches in front of me and knocks the canvas off the easel. It falls sideways and tips onto the floor, paint up. Emerson pulls out and wrenches me down. Puts me on my knees. I catch myself on the canvas. Both hands in the ocean now. For three heartbeats I'm scared, but then his fingers are at work. He pushes back inside. All my dangerous desires return. This is wrong. This is filthy. To be fucked on a painting like this. On the floor. It's good.

I should have known better than to doubt him. He watches me so carefully. He wouldn't do this unless I could take it.

He pulls out, leaving his tip inside, and pauses. Emerson's fingers dig into my ass, rough and unforgiving. I think each fingertip might leave a bruise, that's how hard he squeezes. He's pulling me apart around the head of him, still impaling me. "Your blood is on my cock." His voice is choked. "It's so fucking hot. I've never seen a more beautiful red. Hold on tight, little painter."

Hold on tight, because he's lost control. His strokes rattle me. They shake me. They feel so good. I lift my head up and catch a glimpse of us in the window. I look awestruck, and so does he.

"You're looking at me like I'm art," I say. "You're making me into a painting."

Emerson freezes.

Cold crashes into me like I've done something wrong. He takes one harsh breath, then a second, and his hands are so tight on my hips that it hurts. Not a controlled hurt, either. Not like when he decided to break me open for him. As if he wants to crush me.

"Is that how you feel?" He jerks me upright by the throat. Rough. Uncaring. I whimper with the shock of it. His other hand goes between my legs and he's not easy on me, he's not gentle. "Like you're a piece of art? Something I acquired for my collection?"

I shudder against him. "I can't come again," I try to say, but he doesn't stop.

"I don't care." Emerson forces it out of me. He makes it happen. Pinned against him. His clothes feel like sandpaper. As it peaks, mortified moans spilling out of my mouth, he shoves himself inside so hard I cry out. "You're on display," he murmurs in my ear. "Only for me. In my collection. Only to come around my cock."

Tears leak from my eyes. "Emerson."

But he seems galvanized from my words, as if

the accusation that he treats me like art has made it real. As if he's accepted it as fact. "You're art, remember? I want to see you come, to hear you come. I want to feel your pretty little canvas around my cock."

His muscles bunch as he comes, working to pump himself inside me.

He's painting me. On the inside.

It's hot. I can feel it. What I can't feel is him. There was emotion in the air before, but now there's a strange distance. And…a strange pride. I got what I wanted. I escaped my apartment, and I came here, and I'm not a virgin anymore.

He pulls out of me and I hiss at the sting. His absence hurts, too. As soon as he's gone I scramble up from the floor and turn around to face him. Emerson's on his knees, but there's something wrong with his eyes. They're shuttered. Suspicious.

"Please," I say. My knees are jelly. I can't stay upright much longer.

He stands up and puts his clothes back together. It's a fascinating process. The zipper flashing. The cloth in his hands. *I might fall over*, I try to say. Getting fucked is a lot.

The last thing I feel is his arms going around me. Catching me before I hit the ground.

CHAPTER TWENTY-SIX
Daphne

I RESURFACE FROM sleep with a jolt. In the scramble to catch myself I find the edge of the bed. The sheets feel different. The thread count is way higher than what I have in my apartment.

Which bed is this? Leo's house?

No. I don't recognize the way the moonlight comes in through the windows. It's at the wrong angle. And—I'm not dressed. Not in my clothes, anyway. I'm wearing an oversized t-shirt.

Oh my god.

I'm at Emerson's house.

It's late. I know it's late. I can feel how very late it is. Or very early in the morning. My stomach turns over. A lamp is on, the light low on the bedside table.

I left the light on at my apartment.

I left the light on.

Guilt chokes me first, followed by fear. I left the light on, and the security team will check on me. They'll discover I'm not in my apartment.

No, it's worse than that. They'll have done it already. Leo's new orders mean that when something is out of the ordinary, they have to follow up on it. I almost never leave my lights on all night. One of the bodyguards will have noticed. One of them will have crossed the street and knocked on my door to check. Or they'd notice when I don't leave in the morning.

They already came to check. It's a done deal.

Certainty makes my blood feel cold. I can picture the suited men walking around my apartment with purposeful strides. I can picture them placing the first call.

Leo always answers. He always does. Even in the middle of the night.

The scene flashes into my mind. Leo, sitting at the edge of his bed, rubbing a hand over his face while one of those bodyguards tells him that I'm missing. That I am unaccounted for. I know what his eyes will look like as he understands the news. I know how angry they'll look. How haunted.

Oh, shit. What have I done? I push my hair back from my face in frantic strokes and fumble for my phone on the nightstand. Whatever's happening, I can call it off. I will apologize as much as I have to. I'll go over to his house and talk to him about this. I'll promise never to scare him like this again. I promise, I promise. I'm half awake but the call—it can't wait. It has to happen right now.

My phone's not on the nightstand. There's a small lamp there. It's the one casting the golden glow over this room. It's one of those fancy lamps, the one with settings to adjust it. It's on its lowest setting. Emerson didn't want me to wake up in the dark. He also didn't want me to get paint all over his sheets. My hands are faintly blue, but he must have washed them for me. Which feels...

I don't know how it feels.

My phone is the main problem.

I search the covers. Throw them back and push my hands down to the bottom of the bed. Did I kick it down there somehow? I don't usually fall asleep with the phone in the bed, but then I don't remember falling asleep.

I remember Emerson's strong arms and being more tired than I've ever been in all my life.

Probably from the sex.

It's very tender between my thighs. Part of me melts again, which is awful. I shouldn't be thinking of sex at a time like this, when I have terrified at least one member of my family and probably more. Eva's going to be worried, too.

Maybe even angry. I didn't tell her what was going on with Emerson.

Where is the damn phone?

I sit up and force myself to think. I put it in my pocket at my apartment. I ran out into the alley. Emerson's car. He took my coat once we stepped into his house. He hung it on a hook, next to where he planned to hang his own coat. The phone must still be in my coat pocket downstairs.

Okay. I need a second to get my bearings, and then I'll get up. I have to let Leo know I'm okay. Imagining his horrified shock makes my heart ache.

It makes me feel like such an asshole.

At least the worst didn't happen. This isn't against my will. This was exactly my will.

Emerson comes in through the bedroom door. He's been transformed. He fucked me in his lovely pants and his dress shirt, but now he's very obviously showered and changed. He's shirtless, wearing only loose sleep pants slung low on his hips.

My whole body flushes at the sight of him. He has perfect abs. He has a stunning body. His eyes meet mine, and he smiles a little.

Thank god.

Something happened in the studio, right at the end. It was something I'd said. About making me into art. But his eyes reflect none of the anger I felt in his body. None of the shock. Only a crisp determination, like it's not the middle of the night.

Emerson comes to the side of the bed, a coffee mug cradled in his hands. Wordlessly, he offers it. Wordlessly, I take it. Midnight coffee is kind of weird, but obviously not a dealbreaker. My nerves begin to calm. If he's giving me coffee, it's probably because he wants to ease me back to humanity enough to take me home. It's not a short drive into the city.

Okay.

Coffee. The mug is warm in my hands. Not too hot. It distracts me from the fading panic. Freaking out right now would not be the act of an independent woman who asked to come here.

Pride feels like champagne bubbles. I wanted to come here. For the first time in my life, I did something that was only for me. It felt so good.

That feeling crumples under another wave of guilt. I make a silent promise to myself that I won't do this again. I'll be upfront with Leo about what I want. I'll take this new courage and I'll shape my life around that. Even if it disappoints him.

I hate the thought of disappointing him.

He'll understand, though. He will. Eventually, he'll understand. If it takes a long time, then maybe that's my mistake. Maybe I should have been honest with him.

No more second guessing the past. Enough about Leo. I can't think with all this guilt. I look back up at Emerson and smile.

"How are you, little painter?"

I take stock. "Sore," I admit, my face heating all over again. "But…it was good."

All except that moment at the end.

But we can move past it. From the way Emerson looks right now, he's willing to move past it. Chalk it up to an intense moment during sex. I'm sure people have those all the time.

It's going to be okay.

"You felt good," he says, but it's not a sweet moment. He's looking past me, at the big window. With the light this low I can see the moonlight on the ocean.

Something changes in his expression. I couldn't name it. Couldn't describe it to someone else. It's not a total blankness. But it is….an absence.

Like he's gone somewhere else.

Now that my head is clearer, I look down into the coffee. Not a hint of cream. I put my lips on the rim of the cup and taste it. Yes—sugar. This is just how I like it.

Another prickle of unease tiptoes across the back of my neck.

I've never talked about coffee with Emerson. I'm not sure I've talked about coffee with anyone, except maybe Leo and Eva and the guy at the little coffee shop on the next block. I only go there once in a while. You'd have to be watching very carefully, or interviewing everyone on those blocks, to know this about me.

Emerson knows.

Being a Morelli means paying attention. And knowing who's paying attention to you.

I'll do that, too. I'll pay more attention. I won't lower my guard again.

He nods toward the coffee. "You'll probably need that for what I'm about to tell you."

Alarm sweeps through me. I push the mug onto the nightstand, swing my legs over the side of the bed, and stand up. Something terrible has happened. Something involving my family.

Oh, god, that's what it is. Another emergency.

My security team must have gotten through to Emerson, and now he has to deliver the news. He'll have to be the one to get me back to the city. I'm going to have to leave now. If it's Leo— if something happened to him, and it's because of me—

I force my thoughts to shut up for a second and face Emerson. "What's wrong?"

My voice shakes, but it's better than staying silent. I need more information. I can't be shut out again. I have to know.

"You're not getting your phone back," he says, his voice eerily calm. And definitely determined. "Not until I'm sure you won't run."

Individually, the words make sense. They're simple enough sentences. And Emerson's tone isn't particularly harsh. It's matter-of-fact. In one way, this is a good thing. It means there hasn't been a family emergency. Any emergency, really.

You're not getting your phone back.

"You took my phone?"

"Yes."

Not until I'm sure you won't run. I'm pretty sure my heart is going to fall out of my chest and onto the floor and crack like a glass paperweight.

"What do you mean?" I look Emerson in the eye. I need every available piece of information about what's happening to me right now. Emerson is the only person here. He's the only one with any answers. "What do you mean, until you're sure I won't run?"

My throat closes with fear as he looks at me,

his eyes calm. I see the change in them the moment before he speaks.

I see the way they glint and narrow.

I see the danger there.

Real danger. Like I felt in his body when I made that comment.

It's here in plain sight now. Not hidden at all.

A full-body shiver rocks me back on my heels. Emerson takes note of this. He's always taking note of everything, and now I am the only thing in view.

I'm the artwork in his private collection.

"I want to show you my art, Daphne. I think you'll love it."

"Why?" My lips feel numb. Mouth dry. I haven't been this scared since I found Leo in his office. I didn't think it was possible to feel this afraid about anything else. "Why do you think that?"

"Because you're part of it now." Emerson doesn't smile, but satisfaction lights his eyes. He's so beautiful like this. So terrifying. And his voice—this isn't dirty talk in the heat of the moment. He's serious. "You're my newest acquisition."

Thank you for reading DARK REIGN! We hope you loved meeting Emerson and Daphne! Find out what happens when she fights against his bonds...

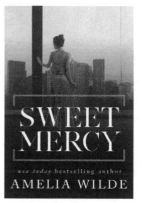

Daphne Morelli is trapped in a gilded cage. She fought to escape her family, only to be caught by a billionaire. Possessive. Commanding. And determined to keep her.

He's determined to own her. She's determined to escape.

In the end only one of them can truly be free.

And if you're new to the Morelli family, be sure to check out Leo's story...

The beast hides a dark secret in his past...

Leo Morelli is known as the Beast of Bishop's Landing for his cruelty. He'll get revenge on the Constantine family and make millions of dollars in the process. Even it means using an old man who dreams up wild inventions.

The beauty will sacrifice everything for her family...

Haley Constantine will do anything to protect her father. Even trade her body for his life. The college student must spend thirty days with the ruthless billionaire. He'll make her earn her freedom in degrading ways, but in the end he needs her to set him free.

About Midnight Dynasty

The warring Morelli and Constantine families have enough bad blood to fill an ocean, and their brand new stories will be told by your favorite dangerous romance authors.

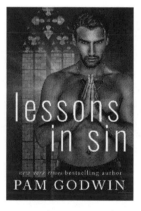

Love forbidden romance with an age gap?

As Father Magnus Falke, I suppress my cravings. As the headteacher of a Catholic boarding school, I'm never tempted by a student. Until her...

I became a priest to control my impulses.

Then I meet Tinsley Constantine.

Haley Constantine will do anything to protect her father. Even trade her body for his life. The college student must spend thirty days with the ruthless billionaire. He'll make her earn her freedom in degrading ways, but in the end he needs her to set him free.

These series are now available for you to read! There are even more books and authors coming in the Midnight Dynasty world, so get started now...

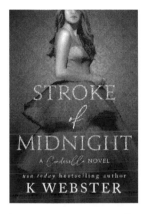

Meet Winston Constantine, the head of the Constantine family. He's used to people bowing to his will. Money can buy anything. And anyone. Including Ash Elliot, his new maid.

But love can have deadly consequences when it comes from a Constantine. At the stroke of midnight, that choice may be lost for both of them.

"Brilliant storytelling packed with a powerful emotional punch, it's been years since I've been so invested in a book. Erotic romance at its finest!"

– #1 New York Times bestselling author Rachel Van Dyken

"Stroke of Midnight is by far the hottest book I've read in a very long time! Winston Constantine is a dirty talking alpha who makes no apologies for going after what he wants."

— USA Today bestselling author
Jenika Snow

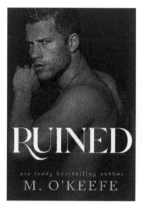

Ready for more bad boys, more drama, and more heat? The Constantines have a resident fixer. The man they call when they need someone persuaded in a violent fashion. Ronan was danger and beauty, murder and mercy.

Outside a glittering party, I saw a man in the dark. I didn't know then that he was an assassin. A hit man. A mercenary. Ronan radiated danger and beauty. Mercy and mystery.

I wanted him, but I was already promised to another man. Ronan might be the one who murdered him. But two warring families want my blood. I don't know where to turn.

In a mad world of luxury and secrets, he's the only one I can trust.

"M. O'Keefe brings her A-game in this sexy, complicated romance where you're left questioning if everything you thought was true while dying to get your hands on the next book!"

– New York Times bestselling author
K. Bromberg

"Powerful, sexy, and written like a dream, RUINED is the kind of book you wish you could read forever and ever. Ronan Byrne is my new romance addiction, and I'm already pining for more blue eyes and dirty deeds in the dark."

– USA Today Bestselling Author
Sierra Simone

SIGN UP FOR THE NEWSLETTER
www.dangerouspress.com

JOIN THE FACEBOOK GROUP HERE
www.dangerouspress.com/facebook

FOLLOW US ON INSTAGRAM
www.instagram.com/dangerouspress

About the Author

Amelia Wilde is a *USA TODAY* bestselling author of steamy contemporary romance and loves it a little *too* much. She lives in Michigan with her husband and daughters. She spends most of her time typing furiously on an iPad and appreciating the natural splendor of her home state from where she likes it best: inside.

For more books by Amelia Wilde, visit her online at https://awilderomance.com.

Copyright

Cover design: Book Beautiful